UNHINGED

I0638413

For information contact :
Wmediaworkscompany@gmail.com
Wmediaworks.com

Book and Cover design by Maurice W
Cover Photography by Maurice W

1

"Maurice W is a master story teller. Unhinged is a fast paced, enormously entertaining, erotic, and sexy read that is almost impossible to put down."

-The Suburban Herald

UNHINGED

Maurice W

W MediaWorks

New York California London

3

For

Joycelyn

CHAPTER ONE

"Fuck! This shit can't be happening…not today of all days," Jason McKay said out loud.

He looked at the clock and could not believe that he had overslept. He remembered setting the wake-up time but forgot to push the alarm button, a mistake that caused the clock to ignore the settings.

"Dammit! That's just what I need, to be late for my divorce hearing," Jason muttered as he leapt out of bed and ran to the bathroom.

Multi-tasking, he brushed his teeth, urinated, and put on deodorant. Since he did not have time to shower, he only concerned himself with camouflaging any funk he may have acquired during the previous day and throughout the night.

Jason peered into the mirror and studied his reflection, contemplating whether or not to shave. Even though his five o'clock shadow threatened an appearance of a ten o'clock, he decided against it since he was already running late. He knew that he could get away with a scruffy aesthetic, confident that he was

8

still just as attractive shaven or unshaven. Standing just a little over six feet, he had the body of a heavyweight boxer. His caramel-toned complexion was smooth and flawless. His clean-shaven baldhead shone as if it were waxed, it drove the neighborhood women crazy.

Dressed down in Sean John attire, Jason made his way to his Acura Legend. He climbed in and sat on the worn beige leather, inserted the key in the ignition and with a turn, the Japanese car began to purr. He marveled at how well the vehicle still ran. Considering that the car was over ten years old it ran better than many of the newer cars available.

Jason ripped onto the street at a fast speed, almost hitting another car as he pulled into traffic. Disregarding the speed limit and most traffic signs, he sped to the courthouse like a man possessed.

It was the month of June and the summer sun beamed relentlessly causing Jason to wish he was pushing a convertible instead of the hot-box he was encased in. He hurriedly pulled into the parking lot of the courthouse and jumped out of the car.

He glanced at his watch. "Twenty minutes late, shit."

Jason ran inside the building and proceeded to go through the metal detector. Now if he only knew where the hearing was being held…

"Where the hell are they," he wondered, rubbing his baldhead. "Courtroom 227, 227. There it is."

He took a deep breath and prepared to enter the room, knowing he would be confronted with his angry soon-to-be ex and her bulldog attorney. Slowly, Jason opened the door and entered. He could feel all eyes turn to him.

The judge glanced at Jason. "Thank you for taking the time to join us, Mr. McKay," he said sarcastically.

Shauna Brandon sat stock-still and said nothing. She rolled her eyes, realizing all the reasons why they were getting divorced and that very moment was one of them. Once upon a time, they were deeply in love but that seemed as if it were another lifetime. After five years of marriage they grew apart. Jason harbored big dreams of becoming a bestselling author and Shauna did not want any part of it. She wanted a husband who got up in the morning, worked nine to five and then came home. No dreams, no ambitions, nothing special. It was because of these differences that the marriage came to an end. Shauna was convinced that Jason was nothing more than a dreamer and she could not bring herself to continue entertaining him. He simply was not the type of husband she wanted.

"I'm sorry your honor," Jason said sheepishly. "I got a flat tire on the way down and my nuts were stripped."

He suppressed laughter, knowing how overboard the stripped nuts comment was.

The judge was unmoved. "Just sit down Mr. McKay so that we could get started."

"Yes your honor, no problem," Jason said, sliding into a chair adjacent to his lawyer.

The lawyer was just a public defendant lawyer sit-in. Jason knew he was screwed the moment he noticed the lawyer glancing at him, desperate for words and direction.

The truth was he would give Shauna whatever she wanted, no contest. The only thing that really mattered was that he could see his daughter whenever he wanted. Anything else was immaterial.

The judge droned on for an hour, but Jason heard none of it. All he wanted was to get out of the courthouse and back to his life.

"Well, what do you have to say Mr. McKay?"

"Huh?" Jason mumbled, the judge's voice yanking him out of his thoughts.

"Do you agree with the terms of this divorce," his honor repeated.

"Yes," Jason said hesitantly, not fully knowing what those terms were. "As long as I can see my daughter then I'm fine with it."

Jason side-glanced his ex-wife, feeling familiar butterflies attack his gut. Damn, she was just as beautiful as the day he first laid eyes on her. Long brown hair highlighted with blond streaks tumbling down her back just past her soft shoulders.

Her features were exotic. Most people assumed that she was a mix of Asian and Black, but in actuality, she was half Cherokee. She had light brown eyes and stood at a supermodel's height. She wasn't but she could have easily been a model if she desired to do so.

Jason knew he had to get used to no longer being married. He accepted that a door had closed and with a sigh, he was ready to begin the next chapter of the story that was his life.

Both Jason and Shauna listened intently as the judge scheduled another court date to discuss the custody and visitation of their daughter, Mercedes.

The judge banged his gavel to signal the end of the hearing. Jason stood up and shook his lawyer's hand before making a quick exit out of the court room. Outside the door, leaned against the wall and pulled a picture of him and his daughter out of his pocket.

"Don't worry baby, daddy will always be there. You can count on that," he said in a low voice.

Jason kissed the photo then placed it back into his pocket before continuing on his way.

16

CHAPTER TWO

J ason hated his job. He had been selling cars for almost two years and even though the money was better than he ever imagined, it was not how he wanted to spend twelve hours of his day. All he wanted was to be at his computer working on the next great American novel, but at this stage that was not reality. There was no profit to be gained in the initial phase of his writing career and he had to do something to keep a roof over his head. Not to mention his other expenses plus he agreed to give Shauna money every week as a kind of unofficial child support.

"Can you help me," asked a soft voice out of nowhere.

He peeled his eyes away from his paperwork and looked up. Right in front of his desk stood a beautiful woman with the most amazing honey-colored complexion. She wore a short haircut that bought her facial features out on display; high cheekbones, almond shaped hazel eyes and full lips.

He loved her eyes the most. As soon as he looked into them, he was entranced.

"Uh…what?" He stammered like an idiot.

She suppressed her laughter, accustomed to getting the same reaction from any man who crossed her path.

Jason regained his composure. "I'm sorry, my name is Jason McKay. Welcome to Toyota Motor World. Um, how can I help you," he asked as he stood up and reached over to shake her hand.

She took his hand with a firm grip then slowly released him allowing her fingers to glide across his skin.

"I'm looking for a used car and everyone else seems to be busy. Can you help me," she asked, peering into his eyes.

Jason's mind started racing as he wondered whether the beauty was flirting with him or not. First off, he refused to make a fool of himself in case she was not flirting. Second, it was better to air on the side of caution. After all, it was rent week and he needed to pay the bills, not flirt with the pretty women who came into the dealership.

"Sure, let's talk a little and find out what it is you're looking for in a vehicle," he said, maintaining a professional tone. "Let's first try and establish your needs."

"Hmm, needs," she repeated, slowly licking her lips looking Jason up and down.

Okay, she's definitely flirting, he thought.

He smiled at her and she shyly looked away. It was obvious that she was attracted to him.

"Let me ask you this, do you have any children," he asked, getting down to business.

As attracted as he was to her, he needed the money and was not about to lose the deal by letting his lustful thoughts interfere with business. Selling cars was something that he was good at and he knew that if he could pinpoint the needs of the buyer then he could lead her to a

21

vehicle that she could not refuse. He was hoping that she did have a child so that he could sell a vehicle's safety feature and make the process more personal. More than anything he tried not to look at her as a woman, but as a buyer. It was tough though considering that it had been months since he had anything that even resembled sex. It was not going to be easy resisting what he believed to be her come-ons.

"Yes, I have a son," she replied, pulling a picture out of her bag.

It was a picture of her and her son at the Jersey shore. He could not help but notice the string bikini she was wearing in the picture. He shifted uncomfortably as he felt his penis harden checking out her toned body.

He gestured towards the seat next to her. "Please," he said graciously, quickly sitting back down in his own seat.

Naturally, he noticed her body the minute he saw her standing in front of his desk, but seeing it almost naked took things to another level. She was roughly about 5"6' and had the body of a dancer. He slid in closer to his desk hoping to keep the bulge forming in his pants hidden. He tore his eyes away from her face and leaned in to look at the picture. As he glanced down at the photo he saw the handsome little boy by her side.

"How old is he," he asked, truly wanting to know.

"Jamir, oh he's five-years-old, four in that picture."

"Wow, he looks just like you, a very good-looking boy."

"Thank you. I'm glad he looks nothing like his trifling father," she said, purposely steering the conversation to her marital situation.

"Oh, are things bad at home?"

"Things are great at home...now that he's gone," she said strongly.

"Divorced?" Jason pried.

"No, he's doing time for murder. He didn't do it, just the wrong place at the wrong time," she said in a low voice looking away from him.

"I'm sorr…"

"Don't be," she interrupted him. "I'm not. He may not be guilty of this one, but he's done enough that he is guilty of. He's where he belongs. When he was home he treated us like shit, so fuck him. I was tired of his ass and left him a week before he was arrested. So, no, don't be sorry. I'm not."

Her words were laced with hatred.

They both sat in silence for what seemed like forever before Jason stood and walked around his desk. He gently put his hand on her shoulder. His touch was warm and it stimulated her.

"Let's go look at some cars for you and Jamir," he said with a grin that could melt the polar ice cap.

25

She smiled back and followed him outside to the used car lot.

"By the way, I never got your name," Jason said, slyly admiring her body as she walked.

"Felicia. Felicia Dennis," she answered in a sultry voice.

"It is very nice to meet you Felicia. Very nice indeed."

CHAPTER THREE

"I'm disappointed. I thought it would be a little bigger, it was just so small..."

Jason's mouth gaped open as Felicia spoke.

He thought that he had pleased her and was shocked to realize that he was wrong.

"You didn't enjoy any of it," he stammered, sounding broken. "Not even a little?"

"I'm sorry," Felicia apologized. "I didn't even enjoy riding it."

That was it. Jason couldn't stand to hear any more. He wiped his brow and climbed to his feet.

"Ok, so tell me what didn't you like?"

"The ride was too bumpy and the car was just too small. I don't think an Acura Integra is the car for me."

Jason, unaccustomed to rejection, felt his ego deflate. He was not used to not picking the perfect car on the first shot. He looked around and then looked at the attractive woman standing beside him.

"Are there any vehicles on the lot that you do like," he asked hopefully.

"What about that Camry over there?"

Felicia moved in the direction of the car.

Jason recognized the look of love written all over her face as she got nearer to the Camry.

He grinned to himself, positive he would close the deal.

The two did a quick walk around and found the car in immaculate condition. It was selling for $18,000 which was $3,000 more than she could afford.

"I love it," Felicia gushed hesitantly. "But it's too expensive. I don't have that kind of money."

"I'll tell you what, let me handle that. I'll tell the big boss that you are my cousin and I'll get the car for you at the price I would be able to buy it for."

"And why would you do that?" Felicia asked demurely, licking her lips.

Jason leaned in. "Let's just say that at the end of the day, I want to be your hero."

The words danced out his mouth before he could stop himself. He winked at Felicia and headed into the office.

Felicia smiled, feeling herself moisten as she thought of Jason. She didn't know why, but hearing this handsome man stand up for her really had her aroused. No one had ever stood up for her before. She knew that she could get any man she wanted. She just always seemed to find men that she would later discover she didn't really want. Maybe this time it could be different. Maybe...

Felicia watched as the men in the office seemed to have a heated conversation. It lasted for about fifteen minutes before Jason returned to his desk where Felicia was anxiously waiting.

"What would you say if I could get the price down to say $15,300," Jason smirked.

"No way! I would say you have a deal!"

"Then let's write it up, because you my dear have a new car."

Jason was happy because he made the deal but what made him happier was the fact that he won some points with this woman that he was beginning to adore.

He glanced at her. "There is a catch however…"

Felicia's smile faded. "I should have known that it was too good to be true. What's the catch?"

"The catch is, I get to be the first person to ride in the passenger seat," he said with a wink.

Felicia exhaled and began to laugh. She was waiting for the worst. She assumed that all kinds of hidden cost were

32

about to be unveiled and was so relieved when it turned out that Jason was just playing with her.

"You got it. I'll give you a ride alright," she smiled, knowing the double entendre would not go unnoticed.

Anyone in the room could feel the chemistry between the two.

As she began to walk into the finance office to finish the deal she turned back to Jason.

"Mr. McKay," she said, seductively. "You are, you know."

"Are what?"

"My hero!"

She flashed another smile before vanishing around the corner to the small office.

33

Jason could barely conceal a grin. He knew they made a connection. When he got back to his desk he noticed that she had left a set of keys on his desk. He slid them into his pocket so that nothing would happen to them.

He didn't know that they were a spare set and unless Felicia was looking for them, she wouldn't even know they were missing.

* * * *

When all the paper work was done, Jason handed Felicia the car keys and opened the door for her. He watched her get into the driver's seat imagining sliding in on top of her.

34

He pushed back the lustful thoughts and pointed out all the necessary controls in the vehicle.

He then kissed her hand, thanking her for the business. The kiss was sensual, letting Felicia know exactly what was on his mind.

"I'll see you Friday night," Felicia said with confidence.

Jason raised an eyebrow. "You will? Do you have to come back?"

"Yes I do. I have to come back to give you a ride. I figure I'll show up around the time you get off and then I'll take you out to dinner. What do you think?"

"I think I'll see you on Friday." Jason bent down and gently kissed the woman's cheek.

"And what time would that be?" Felicia asked, undressing him with her eyes.

"Around nine," he responded quickly.

"Then nine it is," she winked and started the ignition.

Jason watched as the car drove down the dealership driveway and onto the highway. His mind was so stuck on the possibilities that he completely forgot about the keys in his pocket…her keys.

He slowly turned and began to walk back toward his desk.

Smiling to himself, he enjoyed the good day he was having.

CHAPTER FOUR

J ason returned to his apartment feeling wired.

He still couldn't believe what had just transpired. Felicia was a dream. The very thought of her got him hard.

Jason walked around his apartment and began fixing one of the many African masks that adorned the wall. Jason loved African and Native American artifacts and artwork. It was his way of paying respect to his heritage.

Even though he was only twenty-five percent Native American, it was a part of who he was. Dream Catchers, wolf statues, pottery, antique weapons and pipes were all displayed next to African sculptures and photos.

He also did his own wall painting and built many of the home furnishings. The apartment was definitely a reflection of who he was.

Shauna used to say that for a man, he had impeccable taste. Jason credited his style to watching hours of home makeover shows; after all that programming he was bound to pick up some tips.

Jason plopped down on his custom covered couch and lifted his laptop from his unique glass and metal coffee table. He lifted the lid and booted on the Apple computer next clicked on the icon that read ***Book***.

Jason had not opened this folder for almost two months. When the page opened, an empty screen sat before him. He stared at it as he had done every other night since starting. Nothing. No ideas, no concepts, no nothing. Every time he began to write, he would get a couple of paragraphs in and then erase the whole thing.

Jason thought that it would be a breeze, since he always excelled in creative writing in school. This was a far cry away from progress.

One of the main problems that he was having was that he couldn't decide if he wanted to write a novel of fiction, science fiction, adventure, a teen novel or a non-fiction book.

What was it the professor would always say?

He thought of the old advice: *Always write about what you know.*

It was good advice. Jason decided that his mind was completely blank and he couldn't figure it out. Why couldn't he just write? Back in school, he hated having to write about what the professors wanted, yet he excelled anyway. Now that he had

41

the freedom to write whatever he wanted to, he couldn't seem to do it.

Jason knew that he was putting too much pressure on himself and remembered that this was one of the reasons why Shauna had left. She couldn't take all the hours of him locked in a room, neglecting the world, and mentally abusing himself for his failures. Jason hated to fail and he was starting to believe that that was exactly what he was doing.

He stared at the computer for more than four hours without ever hitting a key, other than to switch to the old school Space Invaders video game that he had saved in his hard drive.

That's it, Jason thought. *That is it. I give up.*

Jason couldn't take it anymore and shut down the computer. He stood and walked out of the room. Turning to look at the computer, he cursed it then walked into the bathroom where he began to undress.

Once naked, he looked at himself in the mirror and took notice of his imperfections while simultaneously admiring his form.

He reached down and grabbed the hot water knob and gave it a spin. The water first began to drip then came spouting out like an upside down geyser. Jason liked the water hot and couldn't wait to immerse himself in it. He kicked his clothes toward the door so to not let the water, that was splashing onto the floor, get his discarded clothing soaked. He knew it would be weeks before he did his laundry and didn't want them to get mildewed. He had lost enough of his wardrobe like that already.

The water danced off his skin, soothing his aches and pains while washing off the stink of the day. He was a water person and this he loved. He adjusted the nozzle so that he would be hit with pulsating burst of liquid. He soaped up his masculine form using a natural sponge and scrubbed himself clean. The dirt and exfoliated skin washed down the drain and Jason felt fresher for it.

He reached for his towel and stepped out, drying himself as the water continued to run. He liked to make sure the shower forced as much residual dirt, hair and skin down the drain. It was something he had done since he was a child.

He dried himself and then wrapped the towel around his waist. When he wore a towel like that, he always felt like an Egyptian god. With a glance at his reflection in the mirror, he headed to the palace that was his room.

Leaving all the other lights on, more out of laziness than necessity, he dropped the towel and climbed into bed. There was something about feeling the fabric of the sheets on his skin that soothed him. He considered jerking himself off, but decided sleep was a better option that night. He was exhausted and could use a little shut eye. He turned off the bedroom light, which was just a reach away, and closed his eyes. Within minutes soft snores began and louder ones later followed.

Jason was knocked out for the night.

CHAPTER FIVE

Jason was shocked awake by the sound of the telephone ringing. At first he thought it was part of the dream he had been having about being on safari in Africa, but couldn't understand where a ringing phone would be coming from since regular cell phones didn't work in the jungle. That was when reality hit him and he forced his eyes open

"Who the hell is calling this time of night," Jason grunted as he attempted to answer the phone.

He snatched the receiver up after first fumbling with it. "Yo, who the fuck is this," he demanded sleepily.

"Jason," a soft voice whispered. His eyes opened wide as he began to recognize the voice.

"Shauna? Is that you?"

"Yes," she whispered again.

"Is Mercedes okay?" he asked, now wide awake. He knew that if she was calling at two in the morning something must be seriously wrong. Fear began to overwhelm him.

"She's fine Jay, she's asleep," she purred.

"Jay," he responded curiously.

It had been almost a year since she had called him that.

"Shauna what's going on? It's two in the morning," he said as he glanced at the clock on the nightstand.

She paused for a minute as if she was hesitating.

"Shauna?"

"What are you doing Jay," she asked her velvety soft voice in full volume.

"What am I doing? I was sleeping until you woke my ass up," he said, a touch vehemently. "What do you want?"

"I want you to come over," she replied sweetly.

"You want wha–"

"I want you to fuck me," she said matter-of-factly.

The words seemed to linger for awhile before Jason actually comprehended them.

She repeated herself. "I want you to fuck me! Right here, right now!"

"Shauna…I," once again he began to speak and she stopped him.

"Don't say a word. Just come over. You still have a key, right?"

"Well, yeah I," he stammered.

"Good, just come over."

Before he could say another word, she hung up the phone. Jason was perplexed. He wasn't exactly sure what just happened. All he knew was that he had an invitation to have sex with a woman that he once said was the best he ever had.

Without much thought, he grabbed a pair of sweats from the floor and put them on. It wasn't long before he was semi-dressed and out the door, he didn't even bother to put on socks.

"What am I doing?" he said to himself as he pulled his car from the curb. "What the fuck am I doing?"

He paused for a moment, considering returning to the comfort of his bed, and then hit the gas pedal and continued on his way to Shauna's place. The car moved further away from his home and then seemed to vanish into the darkness of the night.

CHAPTER SIX

Jason stood in front of Shauna's door for fifteen minutes.

He looked at the key, and then moved his glance to the lock and then back to the key again. As horny as he was, he couldn't get himself to unlock the door. Jason began to turn and leave when he heard the lock unhinge. The door slowly opened, and before him stood Shauna in all her glory.

He slowly looked her up and down, first noticing her firm breasts which were slightly hidden behind strands of her long hair. He then moved his attention to her abs, her long shapely legs and then to her sugar spot. Her pubic hair was perfectly trimmed and all he could think of was how he wanted to put his face deep in it.

"Come in," she said as she walked back into the apartment, leaving the door slightly ajar.

As if in a trance he followed her, quietly closing the door. He made his way into the living room, where Shauna stood waiting. She pulled him toward her and gently inserted her tongue into his mouth. In response, his slid into hers.

Her hands found his chest as his danced down her back and made their way to her plump ass. He couldn't help himself, he had to grab it. She gasped with pleasure as she felt his strength. She reached down and began to loosen his sweats pants causing them to fall to his feet. His protruding penis fell into her hand and she grabbed it firmly as if she had grabbed the head of a snake. She felt its size in her hand and then slowly moved her hand back and forth, never releasing his member.

Jason couldn't control himself. He loved the way she stroked him and the way she kissed was enough to make him lose whatever control he had left. He moved to her breast and placed one in his mouth. She threw her head back and moaned with pleasure. His tongue began to dance across her nipple – first circling it, then gently running across it and then moving up and down as his mouth began to suck.

Her nails dug deep into him. She wanted it all from him at that moment. She began to lie down on the carpet and as she lowered herself, she pulled him down on top of her.

During his decent, his eyes met Mercedes' bedroom. Then his eyes involuntarily drifted to the wall where pictures of him, Shauna and Mercedes as

55

a family used to be. She moved the pictures…

Reality hit him like a brick. He was about to have sex with his soon to be ex-wife. Though it wasn't official, for all intended purposes, they were already divorced. The mood was drained from him like a popped balloon losing air. He felt as if someone had punched him in the stomach.

"What is it?" Shauna asked confused.

"I can't do this," he said softly but sternly.

"*What*," she exploded in disbelief. "You got to be kidding me. You got a conscience now? Are you fucking kidding me?"

"Look, we are not together anymore and this shit makes no sense," he said as he pulled his boxer briefs up to his waist and then stepped into his sweat pants.

"You can't leave me like this," she hollered.

"I'm sure you have new batteries, use your toy."

"Are you fuckin kidding me? This is ridiculous," she sputtered, still in shock about getting rejected.

"I gotta go. Part of this was my fault," he apologized. "I should have never come here."

"I don't believe that you are just going to walk out of here leaving me butt ass naked on the floor in need of dick."

He heard her words but kept on walking.

"If I remember correctly, it was you that filed for divorce not me," he said, his words stinging her. "Next time you want some of this dick, maybe you should remember that."

Jason stepped through the front door and closed it behind him. Before leaving, he heard the distinct sound of a vase crashing into the door on the opposite side. He figured that maybe it would be a smart thing to pick up his pace before he shared the fate of the door.

Knowing Shauna as he did, he imagined that she just sat on the floor completely pissed for a moment then she'd get her dildo to finish where he left off.

He knew that as she was pleasing herself, she was also probably spitting out derogatory remarks about him and he was okay with that thought. In total disbelief of what had just occurred, Jason climbed into his Acura and sped off homeward bound.

CHAPTER SEVEN

"Tell me you are lying," Tyrone cracked up laughing.

Tyrone was Jason's best friend they had known each other since the sixth grade. Jason recalled when Tyrone was the elementary school bully who tried pushing Jason around until the day he hit him across the head with a chair, instantly earning the young giant's respect. Tyrone, a massive man of 6' 5" and 250 pounds of solid muscle, always felt that Jason was his one true friend. Jason felt the same way, but as he looked up at his friends darker than dark complexion, he knew he should have kept his mouth shut. He also knew that it was too late to think about that now.

"You walked away from free ass," said Tyrone, still shaking his head in disbelief.

A whole day had passed since the encounter with Shauna, yet Jason couldn't get it out of his mind. He had hoped telling Tyrone would help him get on with his life. He should have known better

61

because now not only will he think about it, but he will also have to listen to the comments that were sure to tumble out his friend's mouth as they sat at the bar's counter.

"You know how I am Ty. When I accept in my mind that something is over, then it's over, period," Jason stated. "Yeah, she was hot as shit and I admit, I wanted to, but what would be the point? So she could call me for a booty call whenever she wanted."

"Hell yeah!" Tyrone grunted as he raised a beer bottle to his lips. "Don't you realize what you have?"

"No enlighten me Ty," Jason said sarcastically.

"You have every man's dream. Sex without the bullshit," Tyrone spat jumping to his feet. "You have a fine ass woman who wants to do you! Who won't ask you what you were doing when you come home late, who won't ask you to wash the dishes or throw out the garbage. Who won't hold sex back from you if you refuse to clip her fuckin' toe nails…oh wait, that's just me, my bad."

"You're stupid," Jason laughed as he finished his screwdriver. "You ever think that maybe I want all of that other shit…well not the toe thing. *That* you can have."

"You're fuckin' nuts," Tyrone belched. "I'd do anything to have what you have."

63

"I bet Tawana wouldn't appreciate that," Jason said referring to Tyrone's wife of three years. "I don't get you. You have a gorgeous woman at home who would give the world to you, and three kids, yet every time I look, you are here at the bar or out playing golf…and you don't even fuckin' like golf. Is it that horrible to go home to your family and spend some time with them? I envy what you have, but it pisses me off that you don't appreciate it. Tawana is a great woman and the kids are precious."

"Oh here we go," Tyrone muttered. "I know being away from Mercedes is tough on you, but stay the fuck out of my business, Jay. I live my life the way I do and though I love ya like a brother, I don't need you lecturing me about how to succeed at marriage especially since, as I see it, marriage doesn't seem to be your specialty."

As soon as he said it, Tyrone regretted his words. "Yo man, I didn't mean that," he tried to apologize.

"No you're right," Jason grumbled. "Who am I to judge? Hey I gotta go. I'll talk to you later."

"Yeah, I hear you," Tyrone spoke as he bumped fists with Jason.

Jason reached into his pocket and removed some bills from a money clip. He tossed the money on to the bar and began to exit the establishment.

"That should cover everything. Tell the bartender to keep the change,"

Jason stated letting Tyrone know all was okay.

"Hey, by the way, how's the book coming," Tyrone said trying a last ditch effort to change the subject. He didn't really want Jason to leave.

"I don't know man. I spent the last two months staring at a blank computer screen. Writer's block and I haven't even began chapter one."

"Damn, that's fucked up. But I know you, you'll make it happen."

"Yeah I know. I just need to know what I want to write about."

"I hear that. You'll get it and when it comes to you, you'll write a best seller then I can quit my job and be your fuckin' manager."

"Yeah, picture that shit!" Jason said heading towards the exit. "Yo, let me get to stepping."

"Alright man. We'll kick it tomorrow," said Tyrone. He knew that there was nothing that he could do to keep Jason from going. However, he really was interested in his friend's writing endeavor.

"No we won't, I think I have a date," Jason said with a wink.

"A date? Oh, you holdin' out on a brotha. With who? You never mentioned a date. You know I live my life vicariously through you."

Jason smirked and shook his head. "Later, Ty."

Thinking about the possible date put a smile on his face. Until that moment, he never believed that Felicia would actually show up. Now it was all he thought about. Before he knew it, he was no longer obsessing on Shauna's booty call. That was the past as was Shauna herself.

He wanted to put his energy in to the possibilities of the future. Jason realized that even if Felicia didn't appear as she said she would, the fact that they flirted the way they did reminded him that there was a world out there and he wanted to be part of it. Jason's mood quickly improved and he began to whistle as he climbed into his car.

CHAPTER EIGHT

Jason couldn't stop looking at his watch.

It was ten after nine and Felicia hadn't shown. He thought that at least she would have called but she didn't. He sunk into his chair feeling disappointed.

"What are you still doing here, Jason? Everybody has already gone

69

home," his corpulent, but slickly dressed boss asked.

"I'm out of here right now. Just finishing up some paper work," he lied.

Jason stood up and double checked his desk so to make sure he wasn't forgetting anything. He turned off his desk light and made his way to the door. His energy level sank as he strolled to the staff parking lot in the back of the building. Jason's mind began to wander. So much so he didn't realize the lights appearing behind him.

"Going somewhere stranger?" Asked a voice from behind him.

Jason quickly spun around and there she was. Felicia had arrived.

"I'm sorry I'm late. I was trying to look good for you," she said with a smile. "My cell phone was dead so I couldn't call. Did you think I wasn't going to show?"

"Well, I'm not even going to lie. I thought you stood my ass up," he said trying to hide his excitement.

"Trust me, I have other plans for your ass…and the rest of you for that matter."

They both smiled at her last comment.

"Hop in, this is my trip," she urged him.

"I need to move my car out so it's not locked behind the gate."

"Don't worry about it, you're not going to need it tonight," she replied, in a syrupy voice. "Trust me."

"Okay, if you say so."

Jason relocked his car and made his way to Felicia's Camry. He paused for a minute and then climbed in. Felicia leaned over and gently kissed him on his lips. His eyes slowly closed as he kissed back. She pulled back and looked at him.

"I wanted to do that from the minute I met you," she said, returning to her driving position. "I hope you don't think I'm being too forward."

"Oh no, be as forward as you want. If you didn't, I would have because I wanted to kiss you from the moment I saw you."

"I hope you like seafood. I made a reservation at this cute seafood place in Manhattan," she whispered.

"I love seafood. Hey," he began to speak then paused until she looked at him. "I'm happy you came."

"I'm happy you are happy," she replied.

Jason fastened his seatbelt and Felicia stepped on the gas. Driving faster than he expected, Felicia weaved in and out of traffic. It was not long before they were driving across the George Washington Bridge leaving Jersey and entering New York City.

Forty minutes after leaving the dealership, they arrived at a tiny yet attractive restaurant on 22nd street. After

73

parking the car, they entered the restaurant and found that the place was bustling with activity.

"Are we going to be able to get a table?" Jason asked.

Felicia walked up to the counter and grabbed the Maitre d's hand, sliding him a twenty dollar bill in the motion and then returned to Jason.

"I'm sure we will get the first table available," she said with confidence.

Almost as soon as she got back, the Maitre d' approached, called their name and began to lead the couple to a private table in the rear.

"Well what do you think," she asked, looking deeply in to his eyes.

"This place is nice," he answered, absorbing in his surroundings. "I've never heard of this place but it's really nice. I like your style."

Jason said as he looked around the dimly lit restaurant. Tasteful nautical paintings graced the walls in an unobtrusive manner. Delicate seascapes and forlorn looking lighthouses dominated the collection. Overhead he noticed fishing nets decorously arranged between the rafters. Antique boat wheels, hurricane lamps and other ship fairing gear were haphazardly arranged around the room, but so as not to distract from the paintings. Among all of this there was one wall that really stood out to him. It was a wall made of weathered wood placed next to a softly illuminated floor-to-ceiling aquarium. Inside the translucent glass swam exotic tropical fish of all colors and sizes. It was like nothing he had ever seen.

The ambiance put Jason into a romantic mood. His attention traveled from the décor back to the woman that sat across the table from him. As he began to stare into her eyes, she continued to speak.

"It's kind of new, but I heard so many good things about it. I really wanted to try it and I'm glad I get to try it with you," said Felicia.

Jason couldn't believe his ears. He knew he was attractive but he never had a woman be so into him so quickly…not that he was complaining.

"Can I get you something to drink while you decide on your meal," a waitress asked as she handed them both menus.

"I'll take a glass of champagne, thank you," Jason requested.

"I think I'll have the same," Felicia purred, seductively licking her lips.

The waitress wrote down what they wanted and then walked away.

"I'm surprised." Felicia said staring at Jason.

"What? Surprised by what?"

"By you," she answered.

"What about me?"

"You didn't look at her."

"Who? The waitress?"

"Yes, the waitress."

"Why would I look at her?"

"Because she's gorgeous. She looked like a lingerie model, kind of like that dim wit…what's her name? Banks, Tyra Banks and the bitch was definitely checking you out."

"Yeah, I guess she did kind of remind me of Tyra. But why would I look at her when I'm here with you, the most beautiful woman in the room. Not to mention, that chick, or Tyra for that matter, couldn't hold a candle to you. If this was "America's Top Model", both would have been voted off a couple of episodes ago and you baby, would go home with the prize," he said trying to reassure her of his attraction while trying to get her to smile.

78

"Ok, you got that," Felicia giggled. "You know, flattery may just get you laid," she said just above a whisper as she seductively ran her fingers through her hair.

"In that case I better start laying it on thick," he said as he reached out and grabbed her hand.

Their eyes met and for a moment, it was as if nobody else existed. Jason got up and walked around the table and bent down and gave her a long, wet kiss. As he began to pull away, she grabbed his head and pulled him in tighter. Their lips locked and their tongues danced until they were interrupted by the sound of applause. The people at the surrounding tables were all staring at them and applauding their

79

open display of affection. Jason returned to his seat and the two began laughing. Just then the waitress returned. She placed the drinks on the table and then pulled out her pad.

"Do you know what you want?" she asked.

Jason and Felicia once again looked at each other and broke out laughing. It became obvious to the waitress, that what they really wanted was each other.

"I'll come back. Get a room," she whispered to herself as she walked away.

"Okay, I'm sorry," Jason apologized to her back while still laughing. "When you come back, we'll know exactly what we want to order. We promise."

"You're bad," Felicia growled.

"You have no idea," he responded in his sexiest voice. "Maybe we should look at the menu. We wouldn't want "Tyra" to freak."

"No, she still has to serve our food and I'm not trying to taste her spit," Felicia said scrunching up her face.

"See, you had to take it there," he laughed. "You just had to take it there."

CHAPTER NINE

"Dinner was amazing," Jason exclaimed patting his mouth with a napkin. "That was some of the best salmon I had ever had."

"See, I told you. What did you think? Did you think that I would take you to Red Lobster or something," she teased.

"Hey, don't knock Red Lobster. All the crab legs you can eat is my idea of heaven," he shot back with a smirk.

"Hmmm, I see I am going to have to raise your standards a bit," she said being as sarcastic as possible. "Obviously, you have no idea of what heaven is."

As the words danced from her lips, Jason felt her shoeless foot invade his crouch. Using her toes, she gripped his penis and proceeded to release, re-grip, release and then re-grip again. Jason was overwhelmed with a mixture of pleasure and paranoia. He was sure that everyone was watching, yet he did nothing to stop its continuance. Felicia seductively traced the rim of her champagne glass with her

pointer finger and said nothing. Her
actions and her expressions said it all.

Jason got the message.

"Do you want to get out of here,"
he asked breathing heavily.

"Absolutely."

Jason reached into his pocket in an
attempt to pay for the meal, but Felicia
stopped him.

"Uh, uh baby. This was my
invitation, therefore my tab," she
explained.

Jason returned his money to his
pocket and nodded in appreciation. This
was a first. He had never had a woman
pay for him before at McDonalds, let
alone a restaurant such as the one in

which they had just dined. Felicia grabbed Jason's hand and the two exited the eatery.

"So what do you have planned for an encore," Jason asked slyly.

"Nothing for right now. I just want to walk around holding your hand and looking into your eyes. Is that okay?"

"That's perfect," Jason said with a passionate smile.

They walked and talked from 22nd street to 34th. They were so into each other that they lost all track of time.

"Wow, look at the time," Jason said completely taken aback as he glanced at his watch which read 2am. "Where did the time go?"

"I don't know and I don't care. All I know is that this was a beautiful evening," Felicia was enjoying the night and hated to see it come to an end. "Let's catch a cab back to the car and I'll get you home," she said reluctantly.

Before she could say another word, Jason grabbed Felicia and pulled her body to his. His aggressiveness got to her. Now she was so turned on that she had to fight herself from ripping his clothes off and mounting him in the middle of the street. Their faces merge as they began to kiss. It was a hard, raw and wet kiss that illustrated the sexual tension that had been building during the evening. Both needed time to catch their breath after they pulled apart. Minutes passed before they spoke.

"I just had to do that," Jason said still trying to recapture his composure.

"I'm glad you did. Damn, I'm glad you did," she said caressing her lips with her fingers.

Jason returned to trying to get the attention of a taxi.

Almost as soon as Jason stuck out his hand, a taxi cab stopped before them. They looked at each other stunned because they knew how uncharacteristic it was for a cab to want to stop for people of color...especially at the early morning hours. They silently decided not to look a gift horse in the mouth and hopped into the rear of the vehicle.

They cuddled like old time lovers as the taxi made its way downtown. The driver couldn't help but to peak into the rearview mirror and watch the couple canoodling and kissing. He almost lost control of the cab as the heat in the back seat began to heighten. Felicia's hand slid into Jason pants and he gasped in delight as she grabbed his stiff manhood. His right hand found its way into her blouse and onto her breast and she began to moan quietly. The passion was so out of control that they completely disregarded the presence of the driver. The cab pulled over upon reaching their destination and the two climbed out never releasing each other. Minutes past, to the frustration of the driver, before Jason pulled out some money and made payment. Jason and Felicia struggled to pull themselves together.

The two lovers climbed into Felicia's car and began their journey back into Jersey. They drove back to Jason's apartment in total silence. Both were so flabbergasted by the power of their attraction they just sat there in the car in need of time to take it all in. After a few minutes of sitting in front of Jason's building they decided to make their way up to the place that Jason called home. They didn't make it to the door before the passion reignited once again.

CHAPTER TEN

Jason struggled to stick it in. He jiggled and wiggled it, but still couldn't seem to get the job done.

The hole was lost to him. Using his right hand, he placed two of his fingers onto the opening which he hoped he could use as a guide still failing to insert his tool.

Felicia was just too much of a distraction, however, not enough of a distraction to cause him to pull his tongue out of her mouth. He continued his attempt and eventually his key found the key hole.

He inserted it and with a twist, the door unlocked. Their intertwined bodies pushed open the door; lost in passion they did their dance from the hallway to the interior of the dwelling.

Once inside, Jason and Felicia clumsily made their way to the couch. They bumped into the coffee table and knocked down an African sculpture.

Without a care, they continued across the floor. Upon reaching the cushioned seat, he gently lowered her body and moved on top of her.

Raw need swirled inside her as he caressed every inch of her body. His stroke was delicate and passionate and it stimulated her until she began to moan. His mouth traveled from her lips to her neck and then down to her breasts.

He tongued her nipples until her body throbbed with a need for release. When she couldn't take it anymore, she pushed Jason back.

"Wait…wait," she said trying to catch her breath. "I'm, I'm sorry. We can't do this. We just met."

Jason pulled back. "What? What happened," he asked, astonished by her abrupt halt.

"Baby, I'm sorry… Look, I like you. I like you a lot and I don't want this to just be about sex," she said hesitantly, unsure of how he would respond.

Lowering himself into a sitting position, he took a deep breath. "I understand," he said sincerely.

Though his actions didn't show it, he actually felt the same way. He had begun to really enjoy Felicia's presence and was starting to hope that she would be around for a while.

"Do you want something to drink," he asked walking to the kitchen.

He needed something cold to relax him. Once in the kitchen he leaned against the broom closet and took a few more deep breaths trying to regain his composure. He then made his way to the refrigerator, opened the door and stood in front of it hoping the frigid air would cool him down.

"Yes. Do you have Coke?"

"Doesn't everyone," he joked.

He removed two cans of soda from the top shelf and popped one open to pour the carbonated beverage into a cup.

As he let it settle in the glass, he reached into the refrigerator again and pulled out the ice cube tray.

He came back to the living room. "Here you go," he said, handing her the cold drink. "So, what now?"

"Can we talk," she responded before raising her glass to drink. "I would really like to get to know you."

"Actually, that is the second best invitation that I've had in a long time," he said, sitting down and placing his hand on her leg.

"What was the first?"

"The first was when you asked me to dinner," he said with a disarming smile.

She smiled back and began to blush.

As the hours past, the two talked about family, life, politics, religion and their prospective sexual histories. They enjoyed themselves so much that they talked until the sun came up.

Jason glanced down at his watch realizing it was six in the morning. He needed to get ready for work.

Felicia glanced at her own watch. "Go hop in the shower and I'll make you breakfast. After breakfast, I'll drive you to work like I promised," she said quickly, not giving him a chance to state the obvious.

She did say that I wouldn't need my car, he thought as he got up to head to the bathroom.

He removed his clothes and climbed into the stream of hot water cascading from the wall mounted faucet.

Using his vanilla flavored bath soap, he lathered his body.

As the water pulsated off of his skin, the events of the night danced through his mind. He wore a huge smile as he submerged his head under the stream of water and continued to prepare himself for the rest of his day.

CHAPTER ELEVEN

"Daddy! Daddy!" Mercedes yelled excitedly, running across the grass field toward her kneeling father.

Jason reached his arms out, ready to catch the incoming torpedo that was his child, his precious little girl.

She slammed into him with such force they both fell over laughing.

This was the way it was every Saturday morning. Both Jason and Shauna had agreed that this park would be the perfect location for the weekly visitation pick-ups and drop-offs since it sat almost exactly in the mid-zone between their residences.

"Hey princess," he said between giggles. "I missed you honey."

"I missed you too Daddy," the five-year-old said grinning her toothless smile.

Mercedes was a mini replica of Shauna. Her light brown eyes and exotic features and were so prominent and pleasing to the eye that people on the street couldn't help but stop and take notice.

Jason, still hugging his child, stood up and began to walk toward Shauna.

Shauna looked like she had an attitude. "Here's her bag. I packed her a dress, just in case you happen to find yourself in church on Sunday. God knows you could use God in your life," she said, handing over the luggage.

"Here we go," Jason whispered. "Religious guilt courtesy of momma Brandon and I have to get the roll over effect."

Jason knew that Shauna had recently been talking to her mother because it was the only time that Shauna wanted to talk about the importance of church. It was one of the things that drove him crazy about her. One moment she's cursing like a sailor, the next she's smoking weed, trying to have sex in a public place. All it took was one conversation from her mother and she suddenly became a wannabe minister.

"What time do you want me to bring her home tomorrow," he interjected, disrupting the sermon that was sure to come spewing out of her mouth.

"Four," she replied. "I have places to be and need her home before I can go."

"Fine."

Shauna stalked off back to her car before Jason turned on his heel to head to his own vehicle. He put Mercedes down and then gently tapped her on the head.

"Tag, you're it," he grinned before running.

Mercedes screeched with laughter and gave chase, pushing her little legs as fast as she could to catch her father.

Jason dipped and ducked trying to avoid his child's touch for a few minutes before making himself trip so that she could catch him.

"I got you, Daddy! Now you're it," she cried happily before she took off running.

Jason jumped to his feet and began to chase her. He let her think that she was actually dodging him out. She would laugh hysterically every time he dived and missed her.

"You're too fast for me girl! But I'm gonna get you," he teased.

As they got closer to the car, Jason grabbed his daughter and lifted her into the air. "I got you, you little chipmunk!"

"Aw dad," she said, collapsing into a fit of giggles.

Jason unlocked the door to his car and helped Mercedes in to her car seat.

As he closed, the door he noticed a car pull around the corner. He recognized it immediately as the car he sold to Felicia a few days earlier.

He waved, hoping to get her attention, but she passed without noticing.

Disappointed, Jason climbed behind the steering wheel and prepared to pull away from the curb.

Suddenly, the same a car, moving in reverse, pulled up alongside him.

It *was* Felicia.

"Hey sexy," she said, brushing a lock of hair from her face. "I thought that was you."

Jason grinned widely. "Felicia! I didn't think you saw me."

"I caught you in my rearview. I had to come by and say hello," she drawled, gazing at him as if she wanted to eat him for dinner. "What are you doing tonight? Maybe we could hook up. I've been dying to make you my homemade Caesar's salad and shrimp scampi."

"Sounds delicious. I wish I could, but I have my daughter this weekend and this is our time," he said, blowing his daughter a kiss.

Felicia arched an eyebrow. "Oh, she's more important than I am," she said, her tone strong.

"What?"

"Baby, I'm joking," she began laughing.

Jason looked relieved. "I was about to say…"

"I got you, didn't I," Felicia said, peering through the window at the child in the backseat of his car. "Well you go and be with her then."

Jason wasn't certain, but he could swear he detected a hint of bitterness in her voice.

"What about Monday," he asked, opting to ignore it.

"Monday it is. I'll call you," Felicia said before disappearing up the road.

Jason pulled off and headed home, his daughter snug and fast asleep in her car seat.

CHAPTER TWELVE

"Daddy, can I have something to drink?" Mercedes asked as she rubbed her tired eyes. "And can you read me a story?"

"Of course I can read you a story. As for the drink, now you know it's too late for you to drink anything. I don't want you having an accident," Jason responded with a half grin.

He didn't want to make a big thing about it, but he was seriously trying to get her to stop wetting the bed. He grabbed his worn torn copy of "Green Eggs and Ham" off the bookcase and made his way to into the bedroom. After making himself comfortable beside his daughter, Jason carefully opened the book to the beginning of the story, and began to read.

"My name is Sam…Sam I am," Jason read with a smirk.

For some reason, this book above all other children's books put a smile his face. Technically, he didn't even have to read a word. By the time he was five, he had every word and rhyme memorized.

He couldn't help but reminisce back to when he was his daughter's age and his mother used to sit in his room and read this book over and over again. As he became a father, he couldn't wait to share the Dr. Seuss classic with her. From the first time she heard it, her eyes lit up. He quickly recognized it as being the same look that he had upon his first hearing the story. Just as he got to the middle of the story, the sound of the phone ringing interrupted them.

"I'll be back princess," he said disappointedly while grabbing the phone.

"Hello? Felicia! Hey baby, let me call you back…I'm just putting Mercedes to bed. I'll call you back when I finish reading her a story."

Jason listened as Felicia paused and responded with an "OK" before hanging up. As he hung up he decided to go into the kitchen and get Mercedes something to drink. He poured about a quarter of a cup of milk into a plastic cup which was decorated with cartoon bees and flowers. It was Mercedes favorite cup. On his way back to his little girl's room, he stopped before the table that the phone sat on, reached down, picked up the phone and gently placed it on the table top. He had no desire of being interrupted again.

Mercedes, faking like she was asleep, popped up.

"Boo," she giggled.

"You scared me," he said with a wink and then handed her the cup.

"Thank you, daddy. I promise to go to the bathroom as soon as I finish. No accidents tonight, I promise."

"OK, we'll see," Jason kissed her on the head as she emptied the cup.

He took the cup and placed it on the nightstand as Mercedes tiptoed to the bathroom. Jason picked up the book and waited for her return. As he waited, he couldn't help thinking about how put off Felicia seemed to be when he told her he had to put his daughter to bed. He was really starting to get a bad vibe, but his thoughts were interrupted by a tiny body slamming into him.

"So where were we chipmunk," Jason said as he re-tucked his giggling daughter into her bed.

111

"My name is Sam. Sam I am. Do you like Green Eggs in Ham," Mercedes screamed with excitement.

"That's right," Jason said as he once again kissed her on her forehead. "Now I want you to go to sleep as I read. OK?"

"Okay Daddy."

"Cool, here we go...I do not like green eggs and ham. I do not like them Sam I Am," he read.

Jason continued to read the book he loved and he knew that he was getting as much joy out of the book as she was. By the time he got to the boat and the goat, Mercedes was knocked out. He listened to her soft bubblegum snores as he turned out the light. On his way out, he spun and looked at her and just couldn't contain his smile.

"Sweet dreams pumpkin, I love you," he whispered while blowing her a kiss that he knew she would never see.

Jason returned to the telephone and picked up the receiver. He began to dial Felicia's number, but couldn't ignore the uneasy feeling he was having. He paused for a moment and then hung up the phone. I'll call her later, he thought. Before he could get five steps away, the telephone began to ring. He instantly recognized Felicia's number. Didn't I tell her I would call her back? Jason thought to himself. He placed the phone to his ear and listened as Felicia began to speak.

113

"Jason its Felicia. Did you just call me?"

"No. I just hung up with you not too long ago and I said I was reading to Mercedes and would call you later, so no, I didn't call you," he said feeling irritated.

"Oh, I'm sorry, I was in the shower and I heard the phone ring. I thought it may have been you."

Jason listened to her words and for some reason knew she was lying.

"I guess your caller I.D. isn't working," Jason said sarcastically. "Look, I'll call you tomorrow. I have a long day before tomorrow and I have many things to do before I go to bed.

"Oh, fine, fine… I'll talk to you tomorrow," she said then hung up without saying goodnight.

Jason retired to his room speechless.

What just happened, he though.

Jason decided that he didn't want to think about it, so he plopped down onto the bed and clicked on the television.

CHAPTER THIRTEEN

"What was I thinking," Jason said to himself as he forced himself to watch the Sponge Bob Square Pants movie.

It was Mercedes' favorite cartoon and she was obviously thrilled to be watching it on the huge movie theatre screen. Jason, on the other hand couldn't

116

stomach the show. He thought that watching the movie version was as painful as sticking needles under his finger nails, but as long as his girl was happy he knew he could endure.

As the movie came to an end, Jason looked over to see the huge smile on Mercedes' face.

"I guess I don't have to ask you if you enjoyed the flick," he stated pleased that she had.

"I love Sponge Bob," she yelled excitedly. "Thank you daddy and I still have popcorn."

"You still have popcorn. Well, we better finish it before you go home. You know mommy doesn't like you to have popcorn."

117

"I know daddy. I won't tell her."

"That's my girl," Jason said with a smirk. "Let's get you lots and lots of candy so when you go home, you can have lotsa energy for her."

Jason knew he was being bad, but couldn't help himself. He just loved sending Mercedes home all hyped up on sugar. The thought of his ex-wife being driven crazy made him smile. Hey, a man could only have so many joys in life.

Suddenly, the phone rang startling them both. Jason pulled out his cellular phone and answered.

"Hello?" he asked. "Felicia? Is everything ok?"

Jason was concerned. He could hear it in her voice that something was up.

118

"Daddy you are always on the phone," Mercedes said with a huff.

"Shhh, hold on honey," he said affectionately to his daughter. "Tell me what is up."

"I …someone broke into my place …I was robbed. Can you come over," Felicia's voice was filled with terror.

"I'll be right over. Let me take my daughter home and I will be right there."

Jason couldn't help but think that there was more to it. He grabbed his daughter and started moving toward the car.

"Is everything okay daddy?"

"Yeah baby, my friend has a problem and I'm going to go help them with it once I take you home."

"What about the candy?"
Mercedes asked disappointed.

"BAM," Jason barked with a huge
grin.

With a quick motion he presented
her with a handful of candy. In his hand
were all her favorites; a box of chocolate
malt balls, a bag of gummy worms, and
two cherry lollypops.

"And you thought I forgot! Oh
silly girl," he said still smiling.

She attacked his hand with an
enthusiasm that only a child could muster.

"Hey little bit, try to leave my
fingers in place okay."

It thrilled him seeing his child with
such joy on her face.

"Thank you daddy, thank you so much!"

"Oh, your mother is going to hate me for this," Jason said in a low voice.

"What did you say daddy," Mercedes asked.

"Nothing baby, I was just saying that I love you and I had such a great time and I'm happy that you had a great time also."

They climbed into the car and after making sure both were fastened in, he hit the ignition and the car jumped into traffic. It wasn't long before he was at Shauna's and Mercedes' apartment.

He gave his daughter a hug and kiss while trying not to seem like he was rushing. Once Shauna opened the door and she took Mercedes in, Jason ran back to the car and sped toward Felicia's place.

CHAPTER FOURTEEN

Jason waited for Felecia to open the door, not sure of what he would find on the other side. It creaked open as if the weight of the world was on it and Felicia, wearing a white wife beater T-shirt and boy shorts, peeked out. She quickly reached out to Jason and took him into her arms. For a minute Jason lost himself in her grasp.

"Oh God! I'm so glad you're here, I was so scared," she cried frantically.

She began crying. Felicia had a way of being over the top, yet coming off authentic and real. Jason hugged her back and then pushed her away from his body so that he could see her better.

"Now talk to me Felicia, what happened," he asked as they made their way from the living room to the bedroom.

"I came in and all my couch cushions were on the floor," Felecia replied while wiping the tears from her eyes. "They went through my drawers and closets…I don't know what they wanted."

"Was anything taken," he questioned showing his concern. "Everything seems to be in order."

"They got my jewelry box! It was the only thing missing," the words tumbled out of her mouth.

Jason remembered the jewelry box that sat on the dresser and glanced over to the empty space where it used to be.

"How did they get in?" Jason asked.

Without a response, Felicia began to kiss him. It caught him off guard, but he enjoyed it and then remembered the reason for him coming over. He pulled back and led her by the hand back to the front door.

"Felicia, how did they get in," he asked authoritatively as he inspected the doorknob and locks.

"I must have left the door open, I don't know. All I know is that they got in," she claimed noticing him looking at her suspiciously.

Her voice dropped in disappointment. "What? You don't believe me?"

Jason pulled her body into his.

"No, no baby. Of course I believe you," he assured her. "I'm here now. Tomorrow we'll have the locks changed."

All he could think of was making her feel safe. Jason couldn't help it. Felicia's beauty had him hypnotized. The sound of her cell phone vibrating on the coffee table startled them both. Felicia jumped at it and snatched it into her hand.

"Hello? Hey girl, hold on," Felicia said recognizing the caller to be Katrina, her best friend.

She placed her hand on Jason's chest and leaned in almost as if she was about to kiss him. Jason prepared for the incoming lip contact when she abruptly stopped and spoke.

"Excuse me honey...give me a minute."

She turned and walked out of the room. Jason knew that it was obviously a private conversation. Wanting to give her the privacy she deserved, he walked into the kitchen, opened the refrigerator and pulled out a can of no-frills cherry soda.

Felicia closed the bathroom door behind her and continued to talk.

"Hey girl, I can't really talk now," she stated in a whisper.

"Oh, oh he's there," Katrina said in a low voice as if he could hear her.

"Yeah, he's here and if I have it my way he'll be here until tomorrow."

"Go handle your shit, girl."

"Okay Trina, I'm out. I'll call you tomorrow, I'm about to get my freak on," Felicia grinned wickedly before disconnecting the line.

She went back to the living room noticing how Jason was still there.

"Is everything okay baby," he asked, genuinely interested.

"Yeah, it was my mom checking in on me. The whole breaking in thing had her worried," Felicia lied.

"Is that where your son is," Jason asked, realizing that the little guy wasn't racing up and down the hallway.

"Yeah, she thought it would be best," she lied again.

The truth was that she had convinced her mom to keep Jamir so that she could have some privacy. As she spoke, she ran her left index finger across the waist band of her boy shorts.

Jason involuntarily licked his lips as his eyes followed its path.

"It is hot in here," she purred. "You have the right idea, I could use a soda."

129

Felicia made her way into the kitchen and Jason followed. His eyes focused this time on her plump, firm ass. She looked so sexy and she knew it, adding an extra wiggle to her walk. The refrigerator door opened, but before Felicia could grab a can, Jason pushed up on her, placing his hardness against her behind.

Startled, she gasped. Jason ran his hands down her body, starting from her head, then moving down her neck, then around her shoulders, and down her side and waist and ending at her thighs.

Goose bumps formed on her arms. Slowly, he leaned in and gently began to kiss the nape of her neck hungrily.

She loved it and threw her head forward for easier accessibility. She reached back, grabbing his bottom the best she could and forced him to press his body harder against hers. The neck and upper spine kissing continued and his hands moved back up her body, never breaking contact, and found her breast. He squeezed and booth enjoyed the pleasure of it. His fingers gently teased the nipples followed by an enthusiastic palming and return to squeezing of her breasts.

The refrigerator's light cast a bizarre shadow of the two bodies on the ceiling that somewhat resembled a dragon. Neither of them noticed. Hips began to gyrate while soft panting and seductive gasps became more frequent.

Jason wanted Felicia and she wanted him just as much if not more. He spun her around so that she was facing him and pulled her away from the cold air of the kitchen appliance. Grabbing her by her wrists, he pinned her to the wall and began to kiss her deeply. His tongue danced slowly in her mouth and hers matched his movement. Her fingers dug deep into his shirt desperate for skin. Like a madman, he ripped his shirt off, not taking the time to unbutton it and without ever removing his tongue from the orifice that it occupied.

Savagely, he grabbed her and lifted her into the air and slammed her down, not too hard, onto the kitchen counter. He removed her panties, spread open her legs and began to caress the inside of her thighs with his finger tips. Felicia, now completely turned on, removed her wife beater and let it fall to the floor. Her nipples stood erect and Jason salivated with wanting. He moved his kiss from her mouth to her neck and from her neck to her breast.

His tongue located her nipples and as his teeth gently clenched onto them, his tongue slowly began to lick in a counter clockwise direction. He continued to lick and suck at the same time and Felicia's body moved erratically as he did.

Felicia moaned loudly now. She reached down as Jason continued to send slivers of excitement up and down her spine. She unbuckled and unbuttoned his pants causing them to fall to his ankles. Her hand grabbed and groped his rock hard member.

Jason sucked in air as if he was taking his first breath. Less than a second past before he returned to the work at hand.

Felicia wrapped her legs around his waist, pulling him closer to her. Her nails dug into his back, drawing blood, as he pushed his hardness into her wet cavern. It was just a tease as he then pulled out and lowered his head to her belly button. Felicia knew where he was headed and was giddy with anticipation. He slowly kissed her skin and began moving south to her sweet spot.

Jason could almost taste her. He licked, teased, and kissed her pubic area and her body jerked with pleasure. His tongue entered her slowly. Her juices were bitter and sweet at the same time. Jason swallowed and drank in what he could.

Grabbing her butt, he forced his face deeper into her hole. Up and down he licked slowly. He knew that she was enjoying it and didn't hesitate to keep the pressure on. He sucked her special spot into his mouth and once again began to inhale, suck and lick. His tongue started off in a counter clockwise direction and then changed direction going clockwise. Felicia's thighs clamped on to his head.

135

When Jason knew that he was bringing her closer to euphoria, he raised himself and once again and inserted his manhood into her. She screamed with pleasure as she felt him between her legs. His throbbing body part caused her to shake and she was loving every minute of it. Her legs wrapped tighter around his body making her look like a child trying to climb a tree. In the excitement, he lifted her up while still inside and using his upper body strength, continued to lift and drop her body onto his shaft. She screamed and moaned with every movement as did he.

Jason gently slammed Felicia against the wall opposite the refrigerator, continuing his stroke. Their bodies picked up speed and was soon pounding into each other. The verbal sounds got louder and louder and sounded as if someone was being assaulted in the apartment. A passerby outside the dwelling considered calling the police as she past and then thought never mind as she continued to her abode.

Felicia's arms grabbed uncontrollably at the wall and then at Jason's body as she got closer to her climax. Jason reached his first with a guttural grunt and then Felicia followed with a grunt of her own that was just as feral. The grunting and screaming continued as both bodies collapsed upon each other. They looked like two Siamese

137

twins having a seizure, convulsing with explosions of pleasure.

"I…WANT…MORE!" Felicia belted out while yanking on his stick like she was milking a cow.

She shoved it into her mouth and began sucking it hard until it magically returned to its stiff stature. Jason was exhausted, but wanted to completely satisfy her. She climbed on top of him and began to bounce. Minutes turned to hours. After four climaxes each and seven hours of body knocking, they both passed out on the kitchen floor.

When they awoke, they were both sore…sore and late for work.

"Oh shit! Look at the time," Jason said, still feeling pain in his body.

His legs felt like spaghetti that had boiled too long.

"I gotta get up," Felicia chimed in.

They looked at each other and once again collapsed onto the floor. They slept for another hour before getting up and rushing out the front door to their prospective jobs.

CHAPTER FIFTEEN

Jason crawled out of bed exhausted. Everything hurt. Six days, Jason thought to himself. I can't believe I've been going for six days. What started off as pleasure had become torture. Six days of what Jason considered the most body blasting sex he had ever encountered. Each night their bodies crashed for nearly seven hours.

Felicia was insatiable and this caused Jason to occasionally fake an orgasm or leg cramp…sometimes both at the same time.

As much as he loved sex and for the most part loved sex with Felicia, he was drained. Together they had done things that he didn't even think was possible, things that he had never done with anyone before.

He looked back at her sleeping form and then moved himself from the bed and limped into the bathroom so he could clean up for work.

When he past the mirror, he caught his reflection for the first time in days. He

141

had seen his reflection, but never truly looked at it. This time he gazed into the mirror as if he was looking for something inside of it other than his face. He noticed his coloring looked strange. It had a pale tan like shade to it with a hint of green. He noticed that he had also lost weight.

I look like a fucking crack head, he thought.

He had climaxed so many times over the last few days that he was dehydrated and his skin looked like that of a corpse that had bled out. What made it worst was that he walked like a man that had just fallen down a mountain, and also felt that way.

He climbed into the shower and began to bathe his body, but could barely tolerate the feel of the water on his skin. Using a plush blue towel, he patted himself dry. Felicia entered and began reaching for his manhood and Jason stopped her.

"Come on baby, I'm already late," he almost protested.

"Fine," Felicia said as if she was being dismissed.

She hopped in the shower and Jason got dressed and made his way to the door.

"Did I do something wrong," Felicia cried out as Jason began to turn the door knob.

"No baby, I'm tired and I'm late."

"You're acting as if you don't want me to touch you."

"It's just that I don't want to start something that I can't finish, you feel me? I can't afford to lose my job, plus aren't you burned out from all the belly bouncing of the last six nights?"

"Yeah, I ache, but in a good way. I love it when I can't walk like this, that means my man handled his business. And you did you know? Over and over and over again. But go, get to work. I wouldn't want you to lose your job because of me," she said sarcastically.

"I'll call you later," Jason shot back.

The door closed behind him and he hobbled to the elevator and pushed the button.

I hope I have a job to go to, Jason thought.

The elevator doors opened and Jason, now forcing his legs to move, got in and he vanished behind the closing metal door.

CHAPTER SIXTEEN

"Jason to the office. Jason McKay to the office," a voice barked with a crackle over the loud speaker.

Jason knew that it was the voice of the general manager. When Frank Gugliatti closed the door behind him, it

146

wasn't difficult to figure out that he was in for it.

"What's up Frank?" Jason asked nervously, trying to act as if everything were okay.

"What's up? What's up?" Frank stood before Jason. "Fuckin' look at you and you want to ask me what's up? *Ma'rone!*"

Frank Gugliatti was a big man. He was articulate and extremely well-tailored, but his demeanor hinted at a past of which he was a wise guy or at least a wannabe. He spoke with his hands when excited and as he spoke to Jason, his hands were all over the place.

"Tell me what's goin' on with you Jay," Gugliati said, more concerned than

147

angry. "You have always been one of my top guys and now you haven't sold a car in a week and you look as if you have been sleeping in the subway."

"I've just been having a rough time getting up and a harder time just ironing my clothes," Jason replied, knowing his response was weak.

"Iron your clothes? It's one thing to not iron your clothes Jay, but to look like you climbed out the dumpster is another thing all together. Not to mention, you wore that same thing yesterday. Are you using?" Gugliatti had to ask.

"Using what," Jason shot back "You mean coke?"

"Yeah, coke."

"If I remember correctly, that was your demon, not mine," Jason barked without thinking.

Two years earlier Frank Gugliatti had a cocaine problem and it was Jason that covered for him and helped force him into rehab. "Oh shit, I'm sorry Frank...I didn't mean that."

"I'll let you get that one. But know this muthafucker, that is the only one you get, do you understand?" Frank took a step back and then walked to his desk to sit down.

"Look Frank, I'm not using. I never have. Well, other than some weed."

"So what is it man? You look like shit and you know you can't be here looking like that."

"Are you firing me Frank," Jason said wounded.

"Don't be a dumb ass," Frank blurted. "You need to go home get some sleep, which you look like you haven't had in weeks and do something about your wardrobe. When you come back tomorrow be ready to make some money and stink a little less *capisce*?"

"Does anyone even say *capisce* anymore," Jason teased now that he knew the worst of it was over.

"Go McKay. I think you should go, now and Jason, you do look like shit."

Jason stepped out the office and a couple of his fellow employees came to him to find out what happened. Jason knew that most of them hoped he had been fired so they could split his pending deals and he had about ten thousand dollars worth on the board.

"Yo Jay, is everything okay?" Barry, the slimiest salesman in the business asked as he grabbed Jason's shoulder feigning concern.

"I'm good, yo," Jason said as he switched into street mode. "I'll be in tomorrow, stay away from my people Barry, you hear me?"

Barry was known for trying to take other peoples customers when they were out because he knew that the deal was closed already and he would still be entitled to half the deal's commissions.

Jason glanced around the room until he found Andy Eagle, the one guy he

151

trusted to talk to his customers. Andy had a gentle disposition and knew how to handle customers.

"Andy, handle any of my customers if they come in, okay?"

"You got it Jay," Andy said enthusiastically.

"Andy, you the man," Jason said with a smile. "Thanks."

Jason tried to swagger but instead wobbled to the car. He climbed into his Acura and decided to sit there for a moment. Jason was so exhausted that after just a few minutes he fell asleep and slept for almost an hour. He awoke to the sound of Frank knocking on his wind shield.

"Take your black ass home," Frank said.

If anyone else would have said something like that, there would have been a fight or at least a lawsuit, but Jason and Frank always made fun of their races in a friendly manor.

"Fuck you, you spaghetti eating guido bastard," Jason shot back and then started the car and drove off waving at his boss.

When Jason got home, he didn't even remove his clothes. He just collapsed onto his platform bed and closed his eyes. The blackness of sleep quickly overtook him.

CHAPTER SEVENTEEN

The sound of the telephone forced Jason conscious.

He reluctantly opened his eyes and reached for the instrument. Clumsily, he knocked the receiver to the ground and then struggled to get it into his hand. Once he got it up to his ear, he spoke.

"Wassup 'Licia," he said after spying the caller ID.

"I called you at work and they told me you were sent home," she said through thick static. It lasted for a second or two before the static faded.

"Yeah. My boss told me I looked like shit and he was right," Jason said, still exhausted.

"Are you blaming me for that," Felicia responded defensively.

"What?" Jason recognized the tone and became confused. "What's with the attitude? No one is blaming you Felicia. Bring it down a notch."

"I can tell you blame me for you losing your job."

"No one lost his job…slow down. I was sent home to get some rest."

"Oh, I'm sorry. It just sounded like you were blaming me for something," Felicia said with less bite.

"I mean, technically, it is because of our sexcapades that I haven't gotten much sleep. And this morning I didn't even have time to change my clothes. I had to go in with what I was wearing, but I don't blame you. I'm a big boy. I could have left and got home at any time and I didn't. So it is safe to say that I'm to blame. Do you feel better now?" Jason felt a need to clear things up.

"Okay baby," Felicia whispered back across the phone lines. "Are you coming over tonight. Jamir will be at my mother's until tomorrow, so I will be alone until then."

"I would love to, but that's the point. I need to get some sleep tonight and you know I will not get any sleep if I'm there, plus, I need to pick up my clothes from the cleaners."

"Fine," she said disappointed.

"By the way, did they ever change the locks?" Jason just realized that he wasn't sure if she did, and if she was going to be home alone, he would feel better knowing they were.

"Uh...yeah," she stated unconvincingly. "Yeah, they were changed a couple of days ago."

"Good. I'll sleep better now."
Jason forced himself into a sitting position.
He looked at the clock and was surprised
to see that is was a little past four in the
afternoon. "I have to go if I am to make it
to the cleaners before they close."

"Fine."

The telephone slammed down
from the other end.

*Did she just get an attitude
because I said that I'm not going to see
her tonight,* Jason thought. She must be on
her period.

Jason jumped out of bed with a
false burst of energy. He ran to the door,
grabbed his keys from the hook that hung
besides the door and then he left. As he
made it to his car, he realized that he

didn't even remember hanging up his keys earlier. He dismissed the thought and blamed his forgetfulness on his exhaustion.

The dry cleaner was just around the corner, but Jason was just too lazy to walk. He double parked in front of the store front and ran inside. He handed a short Korean woman his clothes ticket, she walked over the side of the store and hit a button, and he watched as all kinds of fabrics swished and whirled before him. The woman grabbed a group of clothes when the machine stopped and she brought what she grabbed to Jason. Stapled to one of his suits, was an envelope.

What is this, he thought. He opened it out fell a key.

"Key in pocket," the woman said.

"This isn't my," Jason stopped.

It was Felicia's. He put into his pocket the day he sold her the car. He couldn't believe he forgot all about it.

"You pay now." The woman said abruptly.

Jason rolled his eyes, pulled out his wallet and paid the woman. He thought her attitude sucked, but what was he to do, it was the only dry cleaner in his neighborhood.

Grabbing his freshly cleaned clothes, he hopped into his car and returned home so that he could eat dinner, watch a little TV and go back and get some more sleep. And that is exactly what he did.

CHAPTER EIGHTEEN

Jason punched the numbers and waited for the telephone to ring. It rang four times and Jason was just about to give up when he finally heard a soft voice on the other end.

"Hello Jason," the voice said.

It was Shauna.

161

I hate caller ID, Jason thought. Just once I would like to call someone and they not know it's me.

"What can I do for you?"

"Can I speak to my daughter please," Jason asked politely. He knew after their last encounter that he had to be as nice as possible.

"Yeah, but first, I don't appreciate you sending that girl home with all that candy. When she gets home like that, she is impossible."

Jason knew Shauna was upset and he did all he could do to stop himself from laughing.

"You're not the one that has to deal with her."

"You're right, I'm," he cut himself off, feigning a cough to cover his chuckle. "I'm sorry. I wasn't thinking."

He listened as she huffed and puffed on the other end of the phone line. She called for Mercedes and hearing it, as always, was music to his ears. Seconds passed and then the most angelic voice spoke.

"Hi, daddy! I miss you," Mercedes chirped excitedly.

"I miss you too princess," he said as tears began to welt in his eyes.

It was always the same. He would have thought that after all this time, he would be used to not living with his daughter and in many ways he was. There was something about hearing her voice on the other end of a phone that just took hold of his heart.

"I miss you baby, and you know what…I love you."

"I love you too daddy."

Mercedes loved her father. He was her world and anytime they spent time together or talked, she was in heaven.

"What are you doing sweety?"

"I'm getting ready for bed. Guess what daddy?"

"What?"

"I saw a full moon and it was *bootifal*."

"It was bootifal, huh," he said with a smile, messing up the pronunciation on purpose.

"Yeah, daddy. I wish you could see it too."

"Well let me see," Jason said as he walked to the window.

He was so busy he didn't even realize that it was a full moon. Looking at the moon was one of those special things that they would do together. Jason took a moment and remembered lying in the park with Mercedes and looking towards the sky to stare at the moon and count the stars. Obviously the full moon was their favorite.

"I see it too."

"You do?"

"Yeah, and you know what, if you are looking at the moon and I'm looking at the moon and of course, if it is the same moon, and we know it is…then it's just like we are together," Jason said hoping to make his daughter smile. He knew it was probably more for him than it was for her.

Shauna called out in the background. "Mercedes, bedtime!"

"I have to go to bed now daddy."

"I know, I heard your mom bellow."

"You heard her what?" Mercedes asked innocently.

"Nothing, I heard your mom."

Mercedes began to laugh knowing that her father had said something that he shouldn't have.

"You're silly daddy."

"No, you're silly," Jason replied. "Good night baby."

"See you later alligator," Mercedes said while laughing.

"In a while crocodile," Jason shot back.

"You're an alligator daddy."

"And you're an alligator and a crocodile."

"No, you're an alligator and a crocodile and an *efalant*," Mercedes started laughing hysterically.

She just knew that she had said the funniest thing that had ever been said and that made Jason laugh also.

"Mercedes, don't let me tell you again! Bedtime, now!"

Shauna is such a party pooper, Jason thought. It was no wonder the marriage did not work.

"Goodnight princess," Jason said and then blew her a kiss.

"Goodnight daddy," she blew him a long one back.

They both hung up and Jason continued to look at the moon.

Tonight it was their moon.

CHAPTER NINETEEN

It had been almost a week since Jason saw Felicia and he was looking forward to it. The only physical contact that he had was with "Thelma and Louise", otherwise known as his right and left hands. In the past, this wouldn't have been a problem, but since sexual interaction with Felicia began he found that he needed physical contact.

Tonight Jason had also planned to introduce Felicia to his cooking talent in the form of shrimp scampi, and chicken Marsala. He had stopped at the grocery store and picked up all the ingredients.

I hope she likes chicken marsala, he thought.

If not, he would have it for lunch tomorrow. He laughed to himself as the thought struck him.

Jason realized that it will also be the most time that he and Jamir would have spent together. He knew how much Jamir loved steak and French fries, so he made sure that he had that on the menu. He parked the car and grabbed the groceries from the back seat. He made his way to the door and knocked with his foot. The door opened and Felicia let him in. As he entered, he noticed Jamir hiding behind his mother's legs.

"Jamir, go color," Felicia yelled in a hostile tone.

Jason remembered that Felicia had once told him that she never really wanted children, but embraced her pregnancy with Jamir. She also said that her mother was very strict and controlling with her and it seemed that Felicia was the same with her child. He didn't approve with how she spoke to him and dismissed him, but he knew that it wasn't his place to comment.

"Is everything okay babe?"

"Yeah, why," she questioned.

"Nothing, it was just the way you yelled at Jamir," he couldn't help himself and commented anyway.

"He's been hanging on me since I got home and it's driving me crazy."

Being a parent, Jason understood how a child could wear a person's patience, but Felicia seemed wound too tight.

Jamir disappeared into his room and Jason made his way to the kitchen and began to sort through the bags so that he could cook. Felicia grabbed him from behind and began to kiss him. Jason turned and kissed her back.

At least she seems to be herself again, he thought. She was a little bitchy earlier, so much that he almost didn't come over. He was glad that he decided to come by anyway.

Jason returned to cooking as Felicia watched on. After warming up some virgin olive oil, Jason sautéed some fillet chicken breast, mushrooms, onions and Marsala wine in a shallow sauce pan. The aroma permeated the kitchen and Felicia sniffed it in. She could not believe that he knew his way around the kitchen the way he did.

Jason checked his rice and vegetables and as they reached the end of their cooking, he focused on Jamir's steak and fries.

When dinner was ready, Jason and Felicia set the table together and then

173

placed the food out. Not only did the food smell amazing, the table looked like something out of a magazine. It was obvious that Jason was trying to impress.

"Dinner is served," Jason said with a bow.

"You are an amazing man," said Felicia. "You keep surprising me. I didn't know you could cook like that."

"My mom stopped cooking when I was twelve. It was kind of like cook or starve in our house," he explained. "When I was young, I thought my mother was being mean. But as I got older, I realized that she was teaching her three sons to be able to feed themselves once they were on their own. I can't speak for my brothers,

174

but I began to really enjoy cooking. Today I am hooked on the food network and cooking relaxes me."

"Well, it looks delicious."

"Hopefully you'll feel the same about the taste. Oh wait, I have some White Zinfandel to go with dinner. I know how much you like it."

"You think of everything don't you Mr. Man."

""I try," Jason said with a wink.

"Jamir bring your ass in here and eat," Felicia barked to her son.

Jason thought Felicia's way of calling her son was a little ghetto but decided to dismiss it.

After the meal was over, Felicia cleared the table and Jason took the time

175

to get to know Jamir. Jamir showed Jason his collection of Hot Wheels cars and then the two laid on the floor and played with them for hours. Felicia was surprised at how well they got along.

"I think he likes you," Felicia whispered.

Jason smiled and winked at her and then continued playing.

"Hey can I borrow your phone? My battery is dead and the house phone is getting a lot of static," Felicia asked in her sexiest voice.

"Sure, catch," he responded, pulling the phone out of his pocket and tossing it to her.

Felicia almost dropped it but managed to get a grip on it. She turned

176

and walked out the room while looking at the cell phones display screen. She pressed some buttons as she vanished around the corner. Jason paid her no mind and put his attention back on Jamir.

They were having so much fun that they lost track of time. Jamir fell asleep while pushing his toy on an imaginary road. Jason told Felicia that he would put her son to bed, so that she could relax.

Gladly she did. Jason changed the little boy's clothes and placed him in his bed. As he pulled the blanket up to the child's chin, he couldn't help but think about all the times he had done the same for Mercedes.

"Goodnight little man," he whispered.

Jason made his way back to the living room and collapsed onto the couch next to Felicia.

"You were good with him. Thank you for the whole evening."

"You're welcome babe," Jason leaned in for the kiss and Felicia let him reach his mark.

Felicia then stood up, grabbed him by the hand and led him to her bedroom.

She began to unbutton Jason's shirt and when he attempted to help, she stopped him.

"You took care of me tonight, now it's my turn. You just relax, okay," she whispered in a soft lusty voice.

178

Jason submitted.

She unbuttoned his pants sinking down to her knees as she removed them. Jason's eyes rolled back into his head in pleasure as Felicia began the night of passion by giving him the greatest blow job that he had ever experienced. At that point, Jason knew that the night was going to be a sleepless one…and he was right.

CHAPTER TWENTY

"She's fucked up. You are just too whipped to see it," Tyrone said as he raised a glass of Bacardi and coke to his lips.

"What the hell are you talking about," declared Jason.

"C'mon, are you telling me that you can't tell that this girl has issues. I would put money down, that her place was never even broken into."

Jason shook his head wishing he had never told Tyrone about the break-in.

"Why would you even say that? You don't know her…hell, you never even met her," Jason said defensively.

"Look, did you listen to the story that you just told me. C'mon playa, a little convenient don't you think? Not to mention, you just sat here and told me for the last the hour, that you think she may be jealous of your daughter."

Jason had spent most of the day running errands and then decided to hook up with Tyrone for a few drinks. He spent the majority of the evening talking about Felicia. Tyrone had no problem sharing his opinions with his friend.

"Don't you think it's strange that she would call you when you have Mercedes and when you get over there all she wants to do is screw?" Tyrone asked in his customary vulgar style. "I'm telling you, there is something wrong with that chick…and by the way, I did meet her."

"When?"

"She called me."

"She *what?*"

"The other night. She said you were playing with her son."

"At dinner, when she borrowed my phone. She must have got your

182

number from my virtual phone book," Jason realized, getting pissed at the thought of that invasion of privacy.

"Yeah, whatever," Tyrone dismissed Jason's words and continued. "I asked her where she got my number and she said you gave it to her. I know you well enough to know that you wouldn't give some woman, knowing how jealous Tawana gets, my number for her to call at will."

"What did she want?"

"She said that she wanted to meet and talk about a surprise party that she was planning for you. I was curious so I hooked up with her. By the way...what a piece of ass."

"Forget about what a piece of ass she is, what happened," Jason asked as curiosity engulfed him.

"That's just it. She made no sense. It wasn't your birthday, so I didn't get it. What the hell was the party about? Plus when she spoke to me she seemed a little twisted...it was the eyes. What bothered me even more than that, yes something bothered me more than the creepy twisted eyes. What bothered me more was her insistence to know how to get in touch with Shauna and Mercedes. She just kept pushing to get a phone number and address, wouldn't take no for an answer until she had no choice."

"That number is in my head, I don't keep that on the phone. When she

184

couldn't find it, you think she decided to use the party as a ruse to get the info?"

"Yo dawg, I don't even know what 'ruse' means, but if by that you mean that the bitch was scammin', you damn right," Tyrone finished his drink and waved to the bartender to bring him another.

Why Tyrone? Jason silently asked himself. Of all the numbers on the phone, why would she call him? I never even mentioned him to her. It was as if she was spying on him and knew that Tyrone was his best friend. He realized the absurdity of the thought and pushed it out of his head.

"You ever think that maybe she was really just planning a party and

185

wanted to invite Mercedes and Shauna?" Jason asked, not truly convinced himself.

"You believe that shit if you want. I'm not buying it. I know game and the bitch got game, trust me."

Jason wasn't sure what to think. But what if Tyrone was right?

Nah, that makes no sense. It must be a party. Jason tried not to think about it and ordered a beer when the bartender bought Tyrone's next drink. He pulled out his phone and looked at it as he drank.

Felicia…what the fuck is going on?

A slow moving car passing by the bar caught his attention. It looked like Felicia's Camry, but Jason knew that the bar was way out of her way.

I'm just becoming paranoid, he thought.

The car passed by the bar three times before disappearing.

After more drinks and much more conversation, Tyrone and Jason left the bar and made their way to their prospective cars. An eerie feeling of being watched came over Jason causing him to look around. He didn't notice the Camry parked two rows back. If he did he would have noticed Felicia watching from the shadows.

CHAPTER TWENTY-ONE

Jason couldn't shake Tyrone's words from the previous day. "I would put money down, that her place was never even broken into," Jason remembered Tyrone saying. He knew what he had to do.

Where are they? Where the fuck did I put Felicia's keys?

188

The keys, that he first discovered when Felicia left them on his desk then later appeared at the dry cleaner, was of utmost importance to him on this rainy day.

Here they are. He had placed them on the top of the refrigerator and had forgotten.

Now with them in his hand, he headed out into the weather. By the time he got to the car he was soaked from the downpour of rain. He climbed into his ride, hit the ignition and began to drive. He pulled out his cell phone and called Felicia's job.

She better be there, he thought.

"Hello, Felicia speaking."

Jason was always amazed at how professional she sounded.

"Hey, pretty lady. I had a minute and just wanted to say hello."

"That's so sweet baby. I'm good, busy day though,"

"I hear you. That's why I'm not going to keep you. I just wanted to let you know that you were on my mind," Jason said authentically.

He knew that the call was nothing more than a deception since he couldn't do what he planned to do unless he knew she was at work.

"You are so sweet. Will I see you tonight?" She asked hopeful.

"No not tonight, I promised to take Mercedes to dinner."

"But you just saw–"

"Excuse me?" Jason grimaced as he spoke, not believing her audacity.

"You just saw her, so I thought you'd be free," she relented.

Jason knew that Felicia had caught herself and was trying to correct her statement. Not wanting to make a thing about it, Jason let it go. He had other plans and only had a limited amount of time to pull it off.

"I'll see you on Friday, but I'll call you tonight…be good.

"I'm always good. You be good," she said before hanging up.

As she made her statement, Jason thought about his mission. Be good she says. If only she knew where he was headed, she wouldn't even have said that.

Jason parked his car in front of Felicia's apartment. He paused for a minute, trying to make sure that he wanted to go through with it. He had to and he knew it.

Jason reluctantly made his way to her apartment, reached into his pocket pulling out Felicia's keys. Nervously, he looked around to make sure he wasn't being watched. She said the locks were changed…well, we'll see.

He inserted the first key into the first of two locks and turned it.

CLICK. It unlocked.

Hesitantly, he placed the second key into the second lock and slowly turned it hoping that it would fail. It didn't. The door was now completely unlocked. Jason was disappointed but still thought that there must be a reason why. He couldn't believe that she would lie about something as important as having her apartment broken into.

He entered the dwelling and after a long pause, began to search it. He wasn't exactly sure what he was looking for. Jason searched the living room, the kitchen, and then made his way to the bedroom, all the while trying not to disturb anything. While he was searching the night stand, he came across a picture

that caught his attention. It was of Felicia
and someone he believed to be an ex-
boyfriend of hers. Felicia was dressed in
an evening gown and looked amazing.
She was a beautiful woman there is no
doubt about that.

He placed the picture back where
he found it, before moving toward the
closet. That is where he found the so-
called smoking gun. He was searching the
top shelf when his heart dropped.

On the shelf, just left of a box that
once held a humidifier and behind an
unopened Chia Pet, he found the missing
jewelry box…the same one Felicia
insisted was taken.

Tyrone was right. She had made
the whole thing up just to get him there

the other night. Just to get me to leave my daughter and come to her.

Disillusioned, he exited the apartment.

What do I do now, he thought as he hopped back into his car.

Fucking Tyrone… Jason hated it when he was right.

CHAPTER TWENTY-TWO

Jason knew he had to confront Felicia about the break-in and her lying about it, but he truly didn't want to.

He stood outside her apartment for nearly twenty minutes contemplating his next move. Maybe I'm putting too much emphasis on this, he figured. The problem was that even though there were some things that bothered him about Felicia, he honestly liked her. They had some good times and the sex was off the chain.

"Maybe all I need to do is talk about it and we can get passed this," he said aloud just enough hear it. "God, I am starting to spend too much time contemplating one thing or the other outside this door. I hate this, I'm not sure."

Jason knocked softly on the door, almost as if he was hoping that Felicia wouldn't hear it. That wish was dashed when Felicia poked her head out.

"Hey you, I was starting to think that you were never going to come in," Felicia stated in order to let Jason know that she knew he was out there. "Is everything okay?"

"I have a lot on my mind. I was just trying to work some things out."

Before Felicia could respond, Jamir came running into the room.

"Daddy, you're back," Jamir said enthusiastically as he gave Jason a hug.

"Whoa, little man," Jason said shocked by the little boy's words.

He kneeled down before him and hugged him back before continuing to speak. "Jamir, you know I care about you, but I'm not your father. You have a father. And even if you don't think of him, whoever he is that way, I'm not qualified. Not to mention, I could never be him. That doesn't mean that I don't care for you.

I just don't think it is okay for you to call me that. Do you understand?"

The child cocked his head confused. "But mommy said–"

"Jamir, go back into your room and color. Now," Felicia said before Jamir could utter another word.

"I'm sorry. I told him that I hoped you would become his next daddy," Felicia instantly went into damage control. "I guess he thought that meant that you already took the job."

"Getting a little ahead of yourself, don't you think," Jason said, showing his disapproval of what had just happened. "Look, we need to talk."

He had considered not mentioning his concerns, but Jamir helped him make

199

up his mind. For Felicia to tell that little boy something like that and think it was okay proved that a conversation was truly in need.

They sat on the couch and just as Jason opened his mouth to speak, Jamir re-entered the room. This time he was carrying his coloring book.

"Mommy, Da…," Jamir stopped before finishing to make his comment. "Look, I'm finished coloring."

He put the artwork into his mother's hands and Jason looked on. Jason thought that for a child his age, he did an amazing job and was about to compliment the little boy by telling him so, when Felicia jumped to her feet.

"*WHAT IS THIS,*" she yelled.

She grabbed Jamir by the shirt and pulled him to her.

Shock and dismay fell upon Jason's face. Felicia raised her hand and then slammed it into her son's head causing him to fly across the room.

Jason was too paralyzed to interfere due to his disbelief.

"*What did I tell you about coloring outside the lines?*"

"Hey, what are you doing," Jason yelled, after he regained his composure.

"Jason, please," she shut him down immediately and gave him a stare that said: don't tell me how to raise my child.

Jason got the message loud and clear.

Felicia continued berating the child. "You're my son, and my son doesn't color outside the lines. Only losers color outside the lines. Do you want to be a loser? Because right now that is exactly what you are!"

Jason couldn't believe his ears. It was one thing to push your child to be the best they can be, but this was ridiculous.

Jamir stood up crying his eyes out and gasping for air. He was crying so hard that it sounded as if he was about to have a seizure.

"Now take this book and color another page! And this time *stay inside the lines!* Do you hear me?"

Jamir, now hyperventilating, forced out a sound. "Y-yess."

"What did you say?"

"Ye…yes mo…mommy."

Felicia handed him the book and shoved him toward his room.

Then as if nothing had happened, she sat down and faced Jason. "Now, what were you about to say?" Felicia asked eerily calm.

Thoughts of Dr. Jekyll and Mr. Hyde came to Jason's mind, followed by that of Sybil.

"Yo, he is only five-years-old. What the hell was that," Jason said strongly.

"Yeah, he's five-years-old and if you don't push him for excellence, then he will never achieve it," Felicia responded in full belief of her words.

"Excellence? Hello! He's five-fuckin-years-old! Are you kidding me?" Jason couldn't believe that this was the same woman that he had begun to fall for.

"I know you raise your daughter differently. Excellence obviously isn't the most import thing for you in child rearing."

Oh hell no! Did she just dis my daughter and my parenting skills? Jason wondered.

He was astounded, thinking that this shit couldn't be happening. She wants to make comments about child rearing abilities? What does she not hear herself or is she actually this delusional?

204

"Look lets drop it. Now, what were you about to say," Felicia acted as if everything was okay.

Jason could not comprehend how a person could be so blind to reality. This wasn't the woman that he had gotten to know or thought he had gotten to know. With all he had learned recently, he was starting to see that he never truly knew Felicia. And now that he was finally learning who she was, he realized that he didn't like her at all. Not even a little bit. This was not the kind of person that he would want influencing or being around his daughter.

Instantly, it all became clear as to what Jason had to do.

"I wanted to tell you that I know that you lied about the break-in and the locks being changed. I had also wanted to talk to you about the jealousy that you have of my daughter and the fact that you secretly invaded my privacy by calling a number off my phone without my consent."

This time it was Jason who spoke with an eerie calm.

Felicia got started. "First off, I didn't lie about–"

Jason interrupted her.

"Don't," he stood up before continuing. "The jewelry box is in the closet and the locks are the same as they always were. By the way, here are your keys. You left them the day you bought the Camry."

Jason tossed the keys to Felicia.

Felicia was thrown aback that Jason knew the truth.

He continued talking. "It's all irrelevant anyway. After how you just treated Jamir, actually in the way you treat him most of the time and cap that off with the lies. There is no way."

"There's no way what," she said fearfully.

"Look, if you can act that way with your child, I can only imagine how you would act around mine and you feel obviously threatened by Mercedes. I could have gotten past the lying, but not this. I'm sorry Felicia, but I gotta go."

"What are you saying?" Felicia asked, knowing the answer but not wanting to accept it.

"We're done…breaking up…it's over," he stated.

Jason wanted Felicia to have no doubt in her mind about what was taking place. Before another word could be said, he felt her fist slam into his face causing him to stumble back.

"What the Fuck!" Jason exclaimed holding his chin.

As her second blow approached his jaw, Jason blocked it by grabbing her fist. He then grabbed the other arm just to ensure that her violent tendency was nullified.

"I will ignore the first one, I admit, I didn't see it coming, but I'm not your son. Don't swing on me again," Jason said sternly

"Fuck you Jason. *Nobody* walks out on me! Have you seen me? I'm a fuckin' goddess! We break up when I say so and I say, not today! Nobody breaks up with me."

Felicia had never had a man not want her. She had always had the ability of having the men that she was involved with bow to her every need. She knew her sex was off the chain and that men loved to walk down the street with her on their arm, she was just that fine. As a little girl, her mother would continually put it in her head, that she was superior to everyone

209

else…period. She was taught that she should believe that no matter what.

"Get over yourself *goddess*. You're only making this easier. I wish it was different because I was truly feeling you. And now I know that I didn't even know you."

Jason unlocked the door and without looking back, stepped through the doorway. "Good bye Felicia, I wish you the best."

Jason was barely out when the door slammed behind him. He paused for a minute and let it all sink in. He was feeling relieved and disappointed at the same time, but knew that he had made the only decision that he could.

With a deep breath he continued to his car. Felicia watched him through the window as he drove away.

The look on her face said it all.

This was not over…not by a long shot.

CHAPTER TWENTY-THREE

J ason heard the telephone
ringing from outside his
apartment door. He just knew it was
Felicia and really didn't want to be
bothered. As he entered, he glanced down
at the caller I.D. and was surprised to
discover that it wasn't her. He snatched up

the phone, hoping to get it before the ringing stopped.

"Hey Tyrone, wassup," he said, pouring himself a glass of juice.

"You tell me, your psycho bitch girlfriend has been blowing up my phone for the last hour."

"She *what?* Okay, first let me say that you were right. She lied about the break-in," Jason said defeated.

"It's me, of course I was right. Now why is she calling my ass?"

"Why do you think? I broke up with her and she probably thinks that you can help her get me back."

"You broke up with the crazy bitch? Now, that's my boy," Tyrone

213

cheered on the other end. "Details man, I want the dirt."

"Look, I just decided that she wasn't the woman I wanted to be with."

"Because of the lying?" Tyrone asked.

"No, there was more to it. I would have forgiven her for the lie just for the blow jobs alone it would have been worth it. It was the fact that she abused her son right in front of me and thought nothing was wrong with it. Yeah, the lies and the way she was towards my daughter, the attitude, her personality disorder and of course, her breaking into my phone, these were all unacceptable and reasons to step off."

"I hear you dawg," Tyrone said happily. He was relieved to know that his boy was a free man, once again.

"Yo Ty, I need to just relax, you know? Get over everything that had just happened...let me call you later," Jason said, realizing that he wasn't really in the mood to have a conversation.

"Cool, see you at the gym tomorrow," Tyrone responded hanging up his end of the phone and Jason did the same.

Almost as soon as the receiver was down, the phone rang again. Jason just yanked it up again without checking the number.

"Hello," he said frustrated.

"Daddy...I miss you," the voice said on the other end of the phone.

"Mercedes," he asked uncertain.

It didn't sound like her, but who else could it be?

Then it hit Jason like a ton of bricks. He checked the number on the caller I.D. and realized that it wasn't a number he recognized.

"Jamir?" Jason questioned, hoping his assumption was wrong.

"Yes daddy, please come back. I miss you," Jamir said.

Anger grew within Jason, especially once he heard Felicia feeding the boy his lines. This bitch has lost her fucking mind.

"Jamir, let me talk to your mother."

He listened as the boy told his mom to get on the phone. There was a long pause and then Felicia spoke.

"He wanted to call you...I couldn't stop him," she said sheepishly.

"Are you fuckin' kidding me? I could hear you telling him what to say. Not to mention, is it me or didn't I just break up with you less than an hour ago? Ever heard the expression, clean fuckin' break," Jason said sarcastically.

"Fuck you Jason! This is *not* over."

"Listen to this," Jason said as he slammed down the phone. "Sounds over to me!"

"Ahhh, you gotta love that dial tone. Hope you enjoy it Felicia," Jason said aloud as he entered the bedroom.

How could I have not seen that she was this fucked up? Jason wondered.

He collapsed onto the bed and closed his eyes. The phone rang again. Jason just ignored it and waited until sleep overtook him. It was not long before he was snoring and he didn't wake again until the next day.

CHAPTER TWENTY-FOUR

As planned Jason met Tyrone at the gym. They had put in almost forty minutes of a workout before a noise outside caused everyone to take notice.

"What the fuck was that? It sounded like gun shots," Jason said to Tyrone

"Yeah," Tyrone simply answered.

"Yo, some bitch just unloaded a 45 automatic into a car parked in the parking lot," said one of the gym's trainers.

Everyone in the gym including Jason and Tyrone made their way to the door for a better look.

As people, we are idiots, Jason thought. People hear gun fire and what do they do, run to it and put themselves in the line of a stray bullet.

So du... Jason's thought trailed off at the sound of Tyrone's words.

"Isn't that your car?" Tyrone asked, already knowing the answer.

Jason couldn't even respond he was so in shock.

"Let me guess, Felicia? I told you that bitch was nuts."

They watched as Felicia shot bullets through the windshield, windows, the driver's side doors and the tires of the Acura. When no more bullets were available, Felicia hopped back into her car and calmly drove off as if she had simply left a note beneath the windshield wipers.

Jason could not believe what had just happened. Not only was his car just shot up, he realized that in order to know where he would be, Felicia had to have been following him. This made him think about the Camry he saw that night before and the time he bumped into her while picking Mercedes up from the park those weeks ago.

He realized that none of it was a coincidence.

Just how long has she been tailing me, he thought.

Those thoughts faded fast as he remembered his bullet-ridden vehicle.

"My car!" Jason exclaimed as the other gym members turned to look at him. "That crazy muthafucka shot up my car!"

"Yo dawg, she could have put those bullets up your ass," Tyrone stated reminding Jason of the alternative outcome.

"Fuck this bitch!"

Jason ran outside and raced towards his car to assess the damage. "Yo Ty, let me borrow your car."

"Where are you going?"

"I'm going to find Felicia!"

"Oh hell no," Tyrone barked. "My AC works, I don't need my shit ventilated plus it's a lease, I think they charge a lot of fuckin' money when you turn in a car with what do you call them, BULLET HOLES!"

"C-mon Tyrone, I can't let her get away with this," Jason said sternly.

"Yo, just call the police."

"No I have to handle this my way first."

Tyrone shook his head. "You're being an ass and you know I love you like a brother, but there's no way. There is no way that I am going to lend you my car."

CHAPTER TWENTY-FIVE

Tyrone's BMW began to slow down as it approached Felicia's apartment building.

Jason watched as Felicia, carrying a suitcase and Jamir, climbed into her car. They were fleeing, Jason concluded. She must have thought that he called the police.

"Okay can we go now," Tyrone said, breaking Jason's chain of thought.

"No, I want to see where she is going," Jason responded.

"Oh damn. I knew I shoulda made your ass walk."

"If she could follow me, I can follow her."

Jason slowly stepped down on the gas pedal and followed the Camry as it began to move. Jason did his best to keep a distance while not losing sight of his ex. They drove a short distance before following Felicia onto the highway.

The drive lasted for twenty minutes before Felicia pulled into the driveway of a small house. Jason pulled the car over a few houses down and waited. Felicia got out the car and was met by a couple that he guessed to be her parents. They gave her a hug and then hugged Jamir. Together they all entered the house. Felicia was there to stay for a while.

"This is not the time, we can go," Jason said frustrated before driving off.

As he passed the house, he glanced over at the address and stored it into his mind.

You can't hide, Jason thought to himself. *You can't hide*.

As the BMW entered the highway, Jason's cell phone rang and he immediately recognized the number as that of Felicia's cell phone.

"What do you want," Jason said through his clenched teeth.

"You know what I want. I want things back the way they were," Felicia said nonchalantly.

Jason could not believe what he was hearing.

"You just shot up my fuckin' car! Are you *kidding* me?"

"I was hurt…I did that out of love…I love you."

"Hurt? Love? You could have beat the shit out of the car with a baseball bat like most mental cases, but no, you had to take your derangement to another level."

"Put it on speaker," Tyrone whispered trying to hear the conversation.

"Shut up," Jason grunted, covering up the mouth piece so Felicia couldn't hear.

"Who's that? That ex bitch of yours and your brat?" Felicia questioned angrily. "That's why you want to leave me. You want to leave me for them."

"I left you because you're psychotic loon, which you proved by putting muthafuckin' bullet holes in my fuckin' car and let's not go into all that other shit that dictates that you have your own padded room and hourly pills. You want to know why I left you? Just look in the mirror. Now I'm going to give you a break…I'm not calling the police about

228

you assassinating my car. All I want is to be left alone."

Jason heard a scream of anger from the other end of the line and then it went dead. She had hung up. Jason did the same.

"I think she got the picture," Jason said to Tyrone as he adjusted the rear view mirror and readjusted himself in his seat.

"Yeah sure she did and I'm wearing a pink thong," Tyrone said sarcastically.

"I figured as much but that's more info then I needed," Jason shot back. "Let's get out of here."

The car continued on the highway and Jason felt a sense of relief befall on him.

Maybe Shauna will stay with her parents, Jason thought

Jason's thoughts then went from Shauna to his car. "I hope the tow truck didn't have too much of a problem finding my car."

"Oh yeah, like there are so many cars in the gym parking lot with bullet holes in them. By the way, can I drive my car now?"

"Oh yeah, sorry," Jason pulled over onto the shoulder so that they could switch places.

"You couldn't just let me drive all the way back, could you?"

"I'm paying six hundred dollars a month for three years to drive this car and I want my money's worth so that means me driving, not my bullet holed Hoopty driving friend."

"You're an ass."

"That I may be but at least I'm an ass driving a hot ass car," Tyrone said proudly as Jason just shook his head and threw up his arms in defeat.

"Oh shit, I forgot to call the rental agency," said Jason pulling out his phone.

CHAPTER TWENTY-SIX

J ason climbed out of Tyrone's vehicle and with a nod turned and walked into the rental car office as Tyrone pulled away. They were just about to close, but knowing that Jason was on his way, they agreed that one person would wait for him; Bob Myers was the chosen party.

Jason had called from Tyrone's car and informed the agency of his car's damage and his need for one of their rentals.

"Jason, your car and paperwork is ready," said the man in a burgundy blazer who stood behind the counter.

"Thanks Bob," Jason replied with a smile.

The car rental agency worked with the dealership where Jason was employed. Over the years they had built a solid relationship between each organization's employees.

Jason signed the papers and grabbed the keys. He then walked across the parking lot and found what would be his car for the next five days. After unlocking the door, he climbed into the little burgundy Corolla and fastened his seatbelt.

Once he adjusted to the small vehicle, he began his journey home. He looked at his watch and noticed it was after nine.

I have to call Mercedes and say good night, he said to himself.

He parked the car and removed the cell phone from his pocket.

Missed call? I must have turned the phone completely off when I hung up on Felicia.

Jason checked the number confident that it would be Felicia again.

234

He was surprised to see that it was Shauna or maybe it was Mercedes who called.

He hit the redial button and waited for an answer.

"Jason," Shauna answered the call in a whispery tone.

Immediately, Jason knew something was wrong.

"What is it?" Jason asked, feeling worry sweep over him.

"Where have you been? I've been calling," she said frantically.

"I accidentally turned the phone off. Is everything alright," Jason asked concerned.

"No, everything is not okay…"

"What is it?"

"Some woman keeps calling and saying that she knows you left her for me and Mercedes. She just keeps calling back over and over again, telling me that I will never have you. I told her that I don't want you and she said I'm a fucking liar and if she can't have you, nobody can, not me or Mercedes. Who *is* she?"

"Did you call the police?"

"Yeah, but they said that there was really nothing that they could do unless someone actually committed a crime."

"Goddamn police," Jason said angrily.

"*Who is she?*" Shauna asked again agitatedly.

"She's a girl I met and broke up with recently."

Shauna's phone clicked indicating another call. She clicked over and it was Felicia again.

"You think you can steal him from me," Felicia ranted. "Well you can't! I refuse to let Jason leave me for your ugly skanky ass! That's right, I can see your skanky ass."

Shauna disconnected the call and returned to Jason. "It was her again and I think she's outside somewhere."

"Make sure the doors are locked. I'm on my way."

Panicked, Jason hung up his phone and sped towards Shauna's home. As he arrived, in record time, he looked around for Felicia's Camry. It was nowhere to be found.

Relieved, he made his way to Shauna's apartment. The door swung open as soon as he stepped in front of it. Shauna had been looking out for him through the peep hole.

"Did she come up here?" Jason asked, feeling his heart beat accelerate.

"No," Shauna was obviously shaken. "She called two more times but never appeared. What kind of freak did you hook up with? What kind of freak did you bring into your daughter's life?"

Her words caused Jason to feel guilty. If anything was to happen to Mercedes or Shauna for that matter, he didn't know what he would do.

"Where's Mercedes?" Jason questioned

"She's in bed. She has no idea what was going on," Shauna confirmed. "This is fucked up Jason! Where did she even get my number?"

"You're listed Shauna, anyone with common sense could get your number. Tomorrow, change it and make it an unlisted one, I'll handle Felicia."

A knock on the door startled them both. Jason opened the door but no one was there. As he began to close it, he noticed a folded piece of paper on the ground.

First, he looked around then bent down to grab the note.

"What is it," asked Shauna.

"It's Felicia," he said somberly, returning to an upright position. "Shit, I was played."

"*What?*"

"She had no idea where you lived. She somehow managed to follow me here…I brought her straight to you."

"What does the note say?"

"Here," Jason just handed the paper over to Shauna.

She read the note: *Thanks for showing me where the love nest is. It will never be your new home, you know… Nice Corolla by the way. Maybe I should put some holes in it too.*

"I'm sorry Shauna," Jason apologized.

He knew that he had to do something but wasn't sure what. Not long ago, what he believed to be a blessing, had become the worst nightmare that he had ever experienced. He had put those dear to him at risk.

His cell phone began ringing, startling him once again. He pulled it out, glanced down and recognized Felicia's number. He had to answer it.

"Felicia, what are you playing at?"

"You are so fuckin' high strung! Who the hell talks like that? *What are you playing at*," Felicia laughed as she imitated him.

Jason knew that she was trying to goad him, but he couldn't shake the feeling that she didn't truly understand the seriousness of her actions.

"What do you want Felicia?"

"I want you baby, prove to me that you're faithful to me and I will leave them alone."

Was she serious?

How could she possibly think, after what she had done that they could actually be a couple? Jason took a minute to think and then with a deep breath and a sigh, he answered.

"Fine. Let's get together and talk," he decided, the words leaving a bad taste in his mouth.

"Let's meet tomorrow. I'm kinda tired tonight," Felicia said.

"Fine. I'll call you and let you know where."

"Why not at my house or yours?"

Jason didn't want to be alone with her.

"I'll tell you what, let's meet at the diner, have dinner and see where the night takes us," Jason said, feigning sincerity.

"Perfect, I'll see you there baby," Felicia said satisfied. They both hung up

"You are kidding me, right?" Shauna couldn't believe what she just heard.

"What else am I suppose to do. I can't let her do anything insane. I *have* to meet with her."

"Meeting with her is the insane thing. But, I guess I understand that you

243

have to do what you have to do. I'm not going to lie, I'm scared."

"So am I. That's why I am staying the night."

"You're what?"

"I'll sleep on the couch. Just toss me a pillow. I need to be sure that she doesn't come back…I don't know what she is capable of. "

Shauna agreed and soon both prepared for the night. The evening was uneventful, but Jason didn't sleep. Instead, he kept going over in his head how Felicia went from being who he thought she was to what she had become. He was looking for clues to the transition, because he just couldn't get passed the fact that he didn't see it coming.

It was actually becoming an obsession.

He knew that if he could not figure it out, he would never trust another woman. All of a sudden he found himself missing the time he had spent married to Shauna, but he didn't allow himself to dwell on it…those times were in the past.

CHAPTER TWENTY-SEVEN

The sun rose and hid behind the clouds, but that didn't stop the heat. Jason felt like he was engulfed in it. He breathed in the warm air and then exhaled. He was fully awake now and could hear Shauna moving around in the back room. She always did get up early, he remembered. Because of that he knew he had to get up and put the same shirt from the previous night back on. Jason thought it was inappropriate for her to see his bare chest. He wiped the sweat from his brow and sat up, noticing that he had drooled on the pillow. Embarrassing. He jumped to his feet, turned the pillow over and made his way to the door

He wasn't so worried about seeing Shauna, but it was Mercedes that he needed to avoid. He knew that it would be confusing for a little girl to see her father first thing in the morning so soon after her parents divorced. It was important not to create the illusion that he was back with her mother.

He quietly opened the door and began to step out when Shauna stopped him.

"Thank you Jason," she said appreciatively.

"You're welcome. This is my problem I can't let it touch you guys."

"I appreciate that, but promise that you will be careful."

"I will be as careful as possible. I kind of want to see my daughter grow up, you know."

'I know," Shauna nodded in agreement.

"Look, I must go, I hear Mercedes moving around. Kiss her for me."

"I will."

Saying no more, he continued out the door. He wanted to go back and kiss Mercedes on the head, but knew that he couldn't. Before leaving the building, he paused. As much as he tried to avoid it, he couldn't.

It had been some time since he slept under the same roof as his daughter and her mother, and even though he knew and wanted it to be over, he couldn't fight back the emotions. Tears welted in his eyes and with a quick wipe, he exited the building. Looking around, he made sure the coast was clear as he walked to his car.

He grabbed the door handle and scorched his hand. It felt as if it was on fire. Jason shook it off, tolerating the pain. The heat continued to build and Jason couldn't wait to get in front of the air condition. The seat was hot and the air seemed to weigh a ton.

Today was going to be the day from hell all the way around if the heat was any indication.

It made sense though…tonight he had a date with the devil.

CHAPTER TWENTY-EIGHT

Jason had spent the most part of the day running errands and trying to forget the fact that this night he would be having dinner with Felicia.

I guess this is it, he thought as he parked on the side of the restaurant.

Immediately, he noticed Felicia's Camry parked near the fence. He noticed a random guy parked in a Chevy blazer just one car away from Felicia's.

Jason frowned for a second thinking that the guy looked awfully familiar. Since the stranger's face didn't register he decided to ignore his feeling.

What the fuck am I doing? I shouldn't be here. What the fuck am I doing here? Jason asked himself repeatedly.

He stepped between the entrance doors and Felicia was there waiting. His eye's couldn't help but take her in. She looked amazing. What a waist…

The non-couple made their way to a table guided by a waitress. She handed them menus and Jason hid behind his. He thought about the first time they had dinner and what a wonderful and fun time it was. There was so much passion and attraction then. How things have crumbled. He couldn't stand to even look at her.

The conversation was forced and it was obvious. Jason tried to make it through but couldn't. When the waitress brought the bread to the table, Jason knew that there was no way that he would be able to eat.

"Look Felicia, I can't do this. Too much has happened," he chose his words carefully. "I'm not feeling you anymore...this can't work. I can't stay and I can't make believe that everything is okay between us. It's not and I have no intention of wasting anymore of my life on it. I'm sorry, but that is what's real."

"Are you telling me that you are walking out on me again? You know what? You do that! I don't want you either. Run back to your pigeon. You deserve each other and you all need to go to hell and will," Felicia said, throwing the bread basket at him.

Felicia pulled out her phone as she stormed out.

Jason overheard her say: "It's over."

He was not sure if she was talking to the person on the other end or him. He concluded that she was just trying to have the last word.

Hey, let her believe that she ended it …maybe that way it will finally be over.

Jason called over the first waitress he saw and cancelled their orders. He stood up, reached in his pocket and removed his worn wallet and snatched out a bill. It was a twenty. He left the twenty dollar tip on the table even though they never actually ate anything. He thought it was the least he could do after the scene that was made.

Jason left the diner and felt a weight lifted off his shoulders. With a deep breath, he accepted the fact that Felicia was behind him, a thing of the past.

And if I never see her again, it will be too soon, he thought.

As he approached his car, he noticed that the Chevy Blazer was still there and the familiar face was still inside.

That has got to suck...waiting for a date to show up, I hate that.

Jason jangled his brain wishing he could place the guy's face. For the life of him, he could not remember. He knew that it was going to bother him for the rest of the evening.

The car vibrated to life as Jason turned the key in the ignition. He clicked on the radio and began to drive. As he left the parking lot, he noticed that the Blazer also headed toward the exit.

I guess he gave up, I don't blame him.

Jason drove for about five miles and could still see the Blazer way back in his rearview mirror.

That was when he figured out where he knew the driver from.

"That's the guy from the picture," Jason remembered.

He went back in his mind to picking up a picture of Felicia and a man that day he snuck into her apartment. He wondered if it was a coincidence and decided to test his theory. Randomly, he began to turn up and down unnecessary streets before racing toward the highway.

The Blazer continued to follow.

"Oh shit," he said aloud as the truth became clear.

Felicia sent someone after him because he wouldn't be with her. This bitch must always take shit to the extreme.

Jason figured that he could lose the ominous vehicle, so he put pressure on the gas pedal and the Corolla took off. It became clear that the driver of the Blazer was aware that Jason knew that he was being followed.

It sped up with more speed than the Corolla could muster.

Jason saw the exit coming up so he swerved at the last minute to take it. The tires squealed from the sharp turn causing him to almost miss the road. He heard the skidding sound as the Blazer hit its breaks leaving black smoke behind it.

Jason knew it wouldn't be long before the Blazer caught up to him. He quickly scanned the area and realized that he was blocks away from the warehouse district.

I can lose him in there, he thought frantically.

Without wasting a minute he aimed his vehicle for the group of buildings. As he reached the destination, he began to weave in and out of the warehouse roads and then pulled the car to a stop. He cut the lights and the engine and began to look for some kind of weapon…just in case. There was nothing to find.

Shit, shit, shit.

In his car, he always had a bat under the front seat, but this wasn't his car. He opened the glove box only to find the owner's manual, an ink pen and a compact flashlight. Frustrated, he threw the flashlight down on to the passenger seat.

Jason knew he was in trouble. Out of the corner of his eye he noticed a set of headlights and heard the sound of the Blazer as it got closer to his location. His heartbeat began to beat louder and faster when suddenly he had an idea.

The Blazer pulled up behind him and the driver got out. Jason's fear was enhanced when he saw the man had a gun in his right hand. Jason realized that he could be living his last moments and all he could think about was Mercedes. How was Mercedes going to deal with his death?

As the man got closer to the car, Jason took a deep breath. Felicia's friend yanked the Corolla door open but it was empty.

Jason had already exited the car and had been watching the man from the shadows. It was time for him to make his move.

"Move and I will blow your fuckin' brains out," Jason said authoritatively as he stepped out behind him. "Do it! Make a move, make my day. Turn around and I'll splatter your brains all over this car."

Jason pressed the bottom of the compact flashlight against the man's head pretending it was a gun.

261

"Drop the gun...now!" He barked. "Now take two steps forward."

The man followed Jason's orders. Nervously, Jason reached down and picked up the weapon. He quickly put the flashlight into his pocket and then aimed the gun at Felicia's acquaintance's head.

"I think we need to talk, don't you?"

The man refused to answer. Jason yanked the man's wallet out of his pocket and flipped it open. He removed the driver's license and then tossed the wallet on the ground where the man could see it.

"Craig Williams, 210 Prospect Avenue," he read. "Well Craig, I'll say it again…we need to talk and remember I know who you are and where you live. Do

262

you live with any family, I wonder," Jason felt that he was truly beginning to get in to character now that he had the gun and was in control.

It wasn't long before Jason got Craig to open up. The two men spoke for twenty minutes before Jason hopped back into his car, still carrying the gun, and drove away leaving the man behind.

CHAPTER TWENTY-NINE

Jason knocked on the door of what he believed to be Felicia's parent's house. Without checking, due to her expecting Chris, she opened the door and began to step outside where she could talk to him in private.

"Did you get....," Felicia's words were cut short as Jason's hand fiercely grabbed her by the throat.

He slammed her up against the wall of the ranch style home and then forced her inside. He closed the door behind them and then forced the nozzle of the gun down her throat. Her eyes were wide with fear.

"*Listen to me and listen to me carefully*," Jason said in a low and calm voice. "Are your parent's home? What about Jamir?"

"They are all sleeping," she responded.

"Good, now hear me, if you ever come near me or anyone I care about again, that includes Mercedes, Shauna,

Tyrone and anyone I may meet in the future, I will kill your parents, then Jamir and make you watch before I kill you! Just try me."

Felicia tasted the metal in her mouth and then attempted to speak.

"Mmorplfff…," Shauna mumbled incomprehensibly.

"No, shut the fuck up, there is nothing that I want to hear you say," Jason said abruptly.

Felicia tried to speak again. Jason yanked the gun from her mouth and began to climb the stairs to where Felicia's parents and Jamir were sleeping.

"You don't want to shut up. Maybe watching me snuff your family will do the trick."

266

"No! Please God, no," she cried.

Jason returned to Felicia and forcefully re-inserted the gun into Felicia's mouth.

"One more word from you and I will blow you the fuck away. Send you to the hell you deserve."

Just by looking at Jason's face and hearing his tone, Felicia knew he was serious and that she was very close to having a bullet pierce her skull.

He pushed her onto the floor and began to walk away.

Just outside the door, he turned again to Felicia. "By the way, your boy confessed everything to me which was recorded through my cell phone's message service. I sent it to a friend at the FBI before coming here, just in case you get any stupid ideas. This better be the last time I ever hear your voice or see you. Do you understand," he said once again pointing the gun at his onetime girlfriend.

Once he felt that she got the message, he continued on his way to the car. Jason grabbed the ammunition clip that he had earlier placed under the driver's seat and inserted inside the handle of the gun. Jason had no intention of harming anyone even though he needed Felicia to believe that he would. However, he was afraid that due to his anger he could accidentally pull the trigger.

Jason drove off and viewed Felicia's actions in the rearview mirror. He watched as Felicia fell to the floor crying.

This was a good sign.

Maybe just maybe, she got the message.

CHAPTER THIRTY

S pring was making way for the coming of summer. It had been almost a year since the Felicia incident. Memories danced through his mind, but he was glad that that time of his life was far behind him. He hadn't seen or heard from Felicia since he tickled her tonsils with that gun.

One bad apple shouldn't spoil the whole bunch, he reminded himself.

Jason stood in the middle of the dealerships' showroom and looked around. He was so deep in thought he did not hear the footsteps walking towards him from behind.

"Can you help me," a sweet voice asked him.

Jason spun around to be greeted by a beautiful Hispanic woman.

"Sure," he responded, trying his best to exude charm. "My name is Jason, what's yours?"

"Leticia. My name is Leticia," she said, gently pushing a lock of hair behind her ear.

Even her voice is beautiful, he thought.

Jason quickly noticed that she was not wearing a wedding band.

"My pleasure to meet you," he said. "Now, how can I help you?"

"You can't," Frank Gugliati interrupted coming towards them.

"Oh I'm sorry, were you with a customer," Leticia said apologetically.

"No, he doesn't work here. He used to but that was before he became a big time author. Isn't that right, Mr. Author?"

"Whatever. I'm sorry, he's right. I don't work here anymore. I just found it hard to resist your plea for assistance,"

Jason replied with a sexy yet friendly smile.

Leticia smiled back.

"So you're a big time author, huh," Leticia repeated unbelievingly.

"Well, I'm not big-time," Jason said humbly.

"Sure he is, his book just made it onto the New York Times bestseller's list," Frank boasted.

Leticia's smile widened. "Did it really? I'm impressed. I guess I will have to go out and get it."

"I'll tell you what, I promised to autograph one for Frank here, what do you say about me autographing one for you also," Jason offered.

"I would like that," Leticia said blushing.

She was well-aware that Jason was into her and she was attracted to him as well.

Frank turned to Jason. "Here is your car now, back from service," he said as one of the technicians parked the car in front of the building.

"Give me a second," Jason said before running out to his new Toyota Land Cruiser.

He grabbed two books from the backseat and scribbled his signature in them before returning to the showroom.

He decided to personalize the autograph to Leticia by writing:

To Leticia, may everything you touch be as beautiful as you are. Jason McKay 555-6749.

He handed one copy to Frank and the other one to Leticia.

She grinned when she noticed that he left his phone number inside the book. "Unhinged by Jason McKay... Nice title. I can't wait to read it. Maybe I'll call you and tell you what I think. What do you think about that Mr. McKay?" Leticia asked with a flirty grin.

"Please do," he smiled back. "Please do. I think I would like that."

Leticia smiled again. "Well I have a question. I'm going to assume that your book is about a relationship that goes bad.

Have you ever had a relationship like that?"

"I guess it is safe to say yes, I have had at least one really bad situation," Jason responded.

He almost laughed to himself since the book she was holding was based on his bad relationship with Felicia. All those months of writer's block and all it took was a psychotic woman with delusions of grandeur to give him all the writing material he needed. While writing the story of Felicia and their failed relationship, Jason decided to change all the character's name and camouflage it as fiction. The last thing he needed was for the book to stir the hornet's nest and cause Felicia to resurface.

276

"What about you," he asked her curiously.

"I think we all have, but maybe I'll fill you in on mine one day," Leticia said.

"Maybe," Jason winked at her.

He slowly turned and headed towards his car. At the dealership door, he turned once again and took a moment to take in the place he had once spent so much time.

He turned his attention to Frank and his new acquaintance. "Frank, take good care of her, she's a friend of mine," he said smoothly, stroking his bald head.

"You got it," Frank assured him.

Jason nodded his head in approval. He felt that he could now leave knowing that she was in good hands. As he climbed

277

into his vehicle, the phone rang. He spied the number and knew it was his favorite female.

"Hey baby, I'm on my way. I was thinking ice cream…what do you think, Mercedes?"

"Yeah, daddy! I really want some ice cream. Can we go to Friendly's and get French fries too?" Mercedes pleaded on the other end.

"If you want it, you got it. I'll be there shortly. Ask your mom and her friend Steve if they want to come, my treat," said Jason

He was genuinely happy for Shauna. Steve seemed to be a great guy and perfect for her. Well, at least so far…

"Mommy and Steve said sure, they would love too," Mercedes said excitedly.

"Then I'll be there shortly."

With a beep of the horn and a wave, Jason disappeared down the driveway.

Life is good, he thought. *Life is good.*

* * * *

OTHER BOOKS FROM
MAURICE W

Novels

ZERO TO NONE
(adult)
Written by Maurice W

Youth Novels

OUT OF NOWHERE
(7-14)
Written by Maurice W

Non-fiction

LOVENOTES: TRUE STORIES OF
LOVE AND ROMANCE
(17 – Adult)
Stories Selected and edited by Maurice W

Children's Books

THE BEAUTIFUL THINGS THAT I LOVE ABOUT ME
(early reader)
Written by Maurice W
Photographs by Renita Shepard

I NOW KNOW THAT I CAN BE WHATEVER I WANT TO BE
(Early reader)
Written by Maurice W
Illustrated by Maurice W

I CAN JUMP ON MY BED WITH BALLS ON MY HEAD
(Young Readers)
Written By Maurice W
Illustrated by Adam Rigall

Maurice W, who was born and raised in the Bronx, began to professionally write at a young age. At 17 he launched a neighborhood newspaper and soon after landed a position as the Editor-N-Chief of an international teen music magazine.

His journey has taken him from the publishing industry, to the music industry, to the movie industry and back to the publishing world that he loves.

Maurice W is now a filmmaker as well as the author of fiction, non-fiction, youth novels, and children's books. He lives in New York.

W MediaWorks
New York   California   London